NO STRINGS ATTACHED

CHRISTY MCKELLEN

B

Boldwood

First published in Great Britain in 2026 by Boldwood Books Ltd.

Copyright © Christy McKellen, 2026

Cover Design by Leah Jacobs-Gordon

Cover Illustration: Leah Jacobs-Gordon

The moral right of Christy McKellen to be identified as the author of this work has been asserted in accordance with the Copyright, Designs and Patents Act 1988.

Every effort has been made to obtain the necessary permissions with reference to copyright material, both illustrative and quoted. We apologise for any omissions in this respect and will be pleased to make the appropriate acknowledgements in any future edition.

A CIP catalogue record for this book is available from the British Library.

Paperback ISBN 978-1-83617-046-4

Large Print ISBN 978-1-83617-047-1

Hardback ISBN 978-1-83617-045-7

Trade Paperback ISBN 978-1-80656-154-4

Ebook ISBN 978-1-83617-048-8

Kindle ISBN 978-1-83617-049-5

Audio CD ISBN 978-1-83617-040-2

MP3 CD ISBN 978-1-83617-041-9

Digital audio download ISBN 978-1-83617-043-3

This book is printed on certified sustainable paper. Boldwood Books is dedicated to putting sustainability at the heart of our business. For more information please visit https://www.boldwoodbooks.com/about-us/sustainability/

Boldwood Books Ltd, 23 Bowerdean Street, London, SW6 3TN

www.boldwoodbooks.com

This one's for you, Karen. I've loved growing old(er) with you as one of my best friends. Here's to many more years of friendship.

1

KIT

Tokyo train station is crazy-making.

It seems every human on Earth has decided to visit Japan to see the spring cherry blossom at the same time and we're all heading for the same Shinkansen to Kyoto.

It doesn't help that I'm bleary-eyed after my fourteen-hour flight from London either, even though I managed to get a bit of kip thanks to the brilliant invention of lie-flat beds in first class.

I mean, sure, I could have just had an executive service drive me to my final destination, that's usually how I choose to get around these days when I'm transferring between plane and hotel, but the train is so much faster and I'm pumped to experience travelling at nearly two hundred miles per hour aboard the famous bullet train.

Luckily, the green car is much less busy than the standard-class carriage and I find my seat easily and crank it back to get comfortable, ready for the two-hour journey.

Closing my gritty eyes, I force my thoughts away from the whole shitshow that was meant to be the reason I was here – my, now cancelled, wedding. I'm here to distract myself from all that, though I'm well aware of the irony that the hotel I'm heading to was going to be where we stayed on our honeymoon.

I'm reclaiming it as the place I'm going to get my shit together instead.

Positive thinking. Something my therapist is always encouraging me to practise.

We set off at exactly the time advertised. The Japanese trains are famously punctual, which I appreciate, especially since I'm desperate to have a shower the minute I get to the Vanaheim Grand, one of a string of five-star hotels owned by one of my best buddies, Elliot.

The guy is a phenomenon and a real inspiration.

As the third child of four siblings, brought up by a single mum after his dad died when he was three, he put himself through uni by doing freelance coding jobs – a skill he'd begun teaching himself during his tweens.

Despite his tough early life, the dude dreamed big and after fulfilling his goal of becoming a billionaire through hard work, guile and skill – a journey he brought me and our friend Raffa along on, gaining us entry onto the rich list and changing all our lives – he was able to finance the take-over of what's become one of the most luxurious and sought-after global hotel chains in the world, with sites in Japan, Sri Lanka, the Maldives and St Lucia, to name a few.

Anyway, spending a week or two here in the Kyoto hotel ought to be enough time to sort my head out. Then I can refocus and move on with the new direction I'm taking my life in, now the path I was travelling on has blown up in my face.

* * *

Chloe

Tokyo train station is such a buzz.

Okay, I'm pretty tired after not getting much sleep in my cramped economy plane seat, especially since I was in the middle of the middle row with a restless, bored child on one side of me and an armrest-hogging giant on the other, but I don't care right now. I'm here, in Japan.

Finally.

It's been on my bucket list to visit since I was fourteen and fell in love with Manga and Studio Ghibli movies, and I can hardly believe I'm actually here.

In my daydreams, it's *always* been the place I spend my honeymoon, which is a bit of a shame as my ex-fiancé decided at the last minute he didn't fancy getting married to me after all.

Not that I'm letting that get me down while I'm here.

It's his loss if he's decided marriage to me isn't what he wants.

And there was no way on earth I wasn't coming on this trip. Not when I've saved every extra penny for years to be able to afford to come and stay in the famous Vanaheim Grand Hotel in Kyoto for a few days before travelling back to Tokyo via the Studio Ghibli Park.

Nothing, and I mean *nothing*, was going to stop me.

Not even a failed wedding.

I make my way to where the Shinkansen tracks are, taking a couple of minor mis-turns in the process, what with the barely decipherable signs and hordes of tourists in my path, but manage to get onto the platform I need two minutes before the train I've booked is due to leave.

Arms shaking under the weight, I stow my case on the overhead shelf just as the train begins to move. My heart is racing from the stress of checking I'm getting on the right one and finding my allocated seat in the almost full carriage, and I take a calming breath before flopping into it with a sigh of relief.

Once settled, I close my eyes and wait for my breathing to return to normal, trying not to think about the fact the empty seat next to me should be filled by the guy I've loved since we met at university and who I genuinely thought I was going to be spending the rest of my life with.

My best friend Sadie's voice floats into my head.

Maybe it's for the best? You're free to do whatever you want now.

Yeah. Maybe.

Anyway, like I said, I'm not going to dwell on that. I'm here for some distraction and a change of scene. There will be plenty of time to deal with the reality of it all when I get home. But for now, I'm choosing not to let his betrayal ruin this for me.

Humiliation can take a seat. And serious relationships too. I'm doing *me* right now.

* * *

Kit

I'm seriously impressed by the Vanaheim Grand when I rock up to it in my executive cab.

It's one of Elliot's favourites, so he tells me, and he's spared no expense making it one of the crown jewels of his chain.

Perched high on the gorge above the Katsura river, it has stunning views of the tree-filled banks and the wide expanse of water, which is sitting fairly low at the moment, though still deep enough for boat rides, so I'm told.

I plan on getting a private hire boat to take me along the famous stretch from Kameoka, back to just past the hotel at Arashiyama. I guess I'll do some other sightseeing too, but I'm here mostly to chill. So that's what I'll be doing for the majority of the time.

I have my own private pool in the apartment I'm staying in, as well as a hot tub and a gym, and there's a dining area where I can eat uninterrupted.

So that's cool.

And if I get antsy, I'll head into Kyoto and have a look around. It has good shopping apparently and some decent restaurants where I can eat if I get bored with the food at the hotel.

Michelin-style dining is all very well – and pretty much all I've eaten since hitting the jackpot and getting extremely fucking rich a couple of years ago – but sometimes you just crave the simple comfort of a burger and fries, you know what I mean?

I down the glass of sake they give me at the reception desk while I wait for them to log my passport details and take a moment to look around me.

The reception area is knock-out beautiful, with traditional Japanese dark wooden framed walls and off-white paper-panelled shutter doors segregating the space. And there are flowers everywhere.

Out of the large windows along the back wall I can see the river winding through the trees below us.

Over on the far side of the reception there's a well-stocked bamboo bar and seating area, with those very low tables and chairs they tend to favour here. All the colours are muted and tasteful as hell.

Just like the hotel's owner.

Elliot was always the quiet one in our group of three at university, but when he did speak, whatever came out of his mouth was of the highest quality. Due to his upbringing, he's been used to looking after himself all his life, so spends a lot of time in his own head. It always amused me to see hot women try to get his attention at uni – and after it, only for him to barely register them.

There's a wealth of gold in there though, if you gain the privilege of penetrating his walls, like Raffa and I did.

In all seriousness, I'd put my life on the line for both those guys.

A finger of unease pokes at my brain. Elliot still hasn't replied to the texts I sent him a couple of weeks ago, which isn't like him. When I spoke to his PA, she seemed a little cagey and just gave me some brush-off answer like 'he's taking some time out right now' and claimed he'd given her no more detail than that. I'm not exactly worried about him, he can take care of himself fine, but it's unusual for him not to get back to me quickly.

I fire off a message to Raffa, asking if he's heard from him.

He replies quickly with:

> Not heard a dicky for a while. I'm guessing he's deep inside some complicated new business deal. Or a woman. Hopefully the latter. The dude deserves some fun

I reply:

> My thoughts exactly. How's life with you?

A moment later, I get back:

> Rocking. My step-bro's getting hitched soon though and I'm being pressured by the olds to go along and play nice. Thinking about taking someone v unsuitable for my date for jinks. Got any connects I can tap?

I laugh out loud. This is typical Raffa humour. He's never got on with his stepfamily, who've treated him like shit since his dad remarried when he was nine. He usually makes a point of steering well clear of them all now. It makes me wonder what kind of pressure they're putting on him to make him turn up for this wedding. Or maybe he's thinking of using it as a chance to get some payback. He's not the Machiavellian type, but I wouldn't blame him for making trouble in this instance. He's had to put up with a lot from those fuckers.

I type back:

> No-one comes to mind stat. I'll think on it. Keep me posted, sounds like it could turn into quite the showdown

My focus is pulled away from my phone's screen when a sleek, grey minibus with the hotel's livery pulls up outside the main entrance. A driver gets out to open the sliding door and allow a lone guest to exit.

My stomach does a weird swoop as a sixth sense about the woman who's alighting makes me pay closer attention. There's something unnervingly familiar about her. I can't see the whole of her face because it's partly obscured by a wide-brimmed sun hat, but there's something about the fluid, elegant way she moves, a bit like a dancer, plus the glow of her perfect, honey-coloured skin that grabs me by the throat.

And her mouth.

Wide and plump and sensual. It makes me think about

things I really shouldn't be thinking about in the middle of a public space. Especially because my body reacts accordingly.

There's only one person I've ever met who's had that kind of effect on me. And it's not someone I thought I'd ever see again. Especially not here. Not now.

As if she's sensed my interest, the woman raises her head and looks directly towards where I'm standing staring at her, unable to drag my gaze away.

A hot shiver runs from the top of my scalp all the way to my feet.

No fucking way.

* * *

Chloe

After stepping down from the hotel's shuttle bus, I take a deep breath of the fresh, oxygenated air. It smells amazing here, so earthy and woody.

I wave away the kind driver's offer to wheel my suitcase into reception for me.

I've never stayed in a five-star hotel before, so I'm not exactly sure how to act. Are you meant to tip? I've been told there isn't a tipping culture in Japan, but does that apply to these sorts of hotels too?

I don't want to get it wrong and appear rude or thoughtless, but I also don't want to step on a custom and make anyone feel uncomfortable. It's a bloody minefield.

No wonder rich people seem so uptight.

Thankfully, the guy doesn't give me chance to put my hand in my pocket and performs a friendly, respectful bow before getting back into the minibus.

I grab the handle of my suitcase and turn towards the main doors to the hotel. It's like walking up to paradise. The entrance is a sea of green, or should I say a river, since we're on the bank of one. It's so lush and vibrant and it makes my heart soar to see it.

I love being amongst greenery. The charity I've been working for since graduating from university is heavily invested in rewilding and maintaining and protecting forests and green spaces in the UK, so I live and breathe plants and trees.

The hotel has been built with a lot of wood, helping it blend into the landscape, though I know for a fact that it was constructed many years ago using sustainable sources. It's one of the reasons I wanted to stay here.

Adrian had wanted to book into a place in the middle of Kyoto for the nightlife, but I was adamant I wanted somewhere quieter. I pointed out that we could travel into the city to find the fun, if we were struggling to make our own.

He'd given in to my wants, as he'd always done, being far more laid-back than me. But of course, I realise now that it was more to do with his guilt about the second thoughts he was having about us getting married.

A hot, sickening sort of dismay rises through me, but I push it down again. I have a horrible feeling it's going to take me a long time to trust a partner again.

Hopefully a week here will help lift the heavy malaise that's been dragging at me since the weekend, anyway. I haven't cried yet, but I can feel it bubbling away below the surface.

Distraction is what I need.

As I move towards the entrance doors, they open with a soft swooshing sound and I walk into the reception area, pulling my case behind me.

It takes a second for my eyes to get used to the change in

light as it's a lot more muted in here, but when they do, I realise I'm looking directly at a tall, broad-shouldered man who's standing in front of the reception desk.

He's staring right back at me.

There's something oddly familiar about him.

My whole body gives a shiver, sending an electric sort of tingle across my skin, as my mind clicks together the pieces of memory I need to form the information I'm grasping for.

Oh my God.

Kit Charleston.

Of all the places and times to see him again. Seriously, karma? Right *now*?

* * *

Kit

What are the odds of Chloe Dasher turning up here, on the other side of the *world*, just when I'm trying to avoid thinking about anything from my past?

I came all the way here precisely to get away from England, in order to get my head straight, but seeing Chloe has brought all the feelings I thought I'd left there rushing back to the forefront of my mind.

Is this holiday going to turn out to be some Scrooge-type scenario? Girlfriends past, present and future coming to fuck with me?

'Hello, stranger,' I say as she walks up to where I'm standing at the reception desk.

'I thought I was hallucinating there for a second,' she says by way of reply, shaking her head in wonder.

'Nope. It's really me. In the flesh. Bumping into you, in *Japan* of all places, after not seeing you for, what? Five years?'

'Second year of university, right? So yeah. About five years.'

A memory of us fucking flashes through my head. We'd been dynamite together in the sack. We'd had a certain type of chemistry I've not been able to reproduce with anyone else. Not even Katya, though it was a different kind of vibe I'd had with her. Don't get me wrong, the sex was great. Just not as *electric* as it had been with Chloe.

And you need more than sex to make a long-term relationship last, as she and I discovered five years ago.

We'd had a lot of fun together at the time though. I don't think I've ever met anyone as headstrong and forthright as Chloe. She always said really left-field things, stuff I never heard coming out of anyone else's mouth, and it had fascinated me. I'd loved how unpredictable she was. It became clear we weren't that compatible, on an emotional level, because she'd been after a more committed kind of relationship, so it had blown itself out after a few months together. We'd parted on fairly decent terms but had run in different social circles, and she'd got together with some other guy pretty quickly after we split, so I'd honestly never expected to see her again.

'So, what brings you to Japan?' I ask, hoping, the moment after I've said it, that she doesn't ask me the same thing. I don't really want to get into the whole cancelled wedding shitshow with her right now. If she does ask, I'm just going to say I'm here to get some R&R after a heavy work stint. She'll never know it's not entirely accurate. We don't have any mutual friends or acquaintances any more so she's unlikely to have heard about my situation.

Chloe visibly swallows and something that looks a lot like sadness flashes across her face.

How weird.

I hope no-one died.

There's a heavy pause before she gives me a strained smile and says, 'This was meant to be my honeymoon, but the wedding didn't happen. I came anyway for a holiday.'

Her honesty knocks the wind out of me.

Well hell, I can't very well lie to her now about why I'm here. Not when she's just trusted me with that.

So I say, 'Snap.'

She frowns and wrinkles her freckle-scattered nose at me. Yeah, she's still as pretty as she was when I last saw her, prettier even. In fact if anything, she's grown more into her looks, which are now verging on beautiful.

Damn it. I really shouldn't be noticing things like that right now.

'What do you mean, *snap*?' she asks, sounding confused.

'I mean, snap, me too.'

She shakes her head, still baffled it seems. 'You too *what*?'

'I was meant to be here on my honeymoon too.'

This time her mouth falls open, and she stares at me in shock. 'Are you *kidding*?'

'Why would I kid about something like that?'

An expression of remorse crosses her face. 'Shit. Sorry, I don't know why I said that. I guess the whole being abandoned at the alter thing has left me with trust issues.' She flashes an apologetic smile. 'And I'm a bit freaked out about seeing you here, if I'm honest. It's made my head spin. Plus I'm jetlagged, so a triple whammy.'

I nod. 'Yeah, me too. It's a long flight from London.'

'So you're here for a holiday too?' she asks.

'Yup.'

'And you're on your own?'

'I am.'

'How are you finding that? I always had you pegged as an extrovert who needs to have people around to give you energy.'

'To give me attention, you mean,' I say wryly, harking back to a conversation we'd had years ago. 'Actually, I just got here myself,' I say, before she has a chance to reply. 'But I'm looking forward to having some time on my own.'

'Really?' Her tone is full of disbelief.

'Yes, really. I can spend time on my own you know. I'm not *that* shallow,' I joke.

She holds up both hands, palms forward. 'Sorry. I didn't mean to imply that you were.' She clears her throat. 'So, what happened to your relationship? If you don't mind me asking?'

I fold my arms and shrug. 'She – Katya – decided I wasn't the guy she wanted to get hitched to after all.'

She gives a little hiccoughy sort of laugh. 'Snap.'

This time I give *her* a questioning frown.

A sad smile plays about her gorgeous mouth. 'My ex-fiancé realised he was in love with a guy he works with and not with me after all. So he dumped me for him. Wedding cancelled. Life reset.'

'Oh shit.'

'Yeah. Not the happy ever after I was hoping for.'

'You know that doesn't really exist, don't you? This whole idea of "the perfect relationship" is just a vehicle for selling romantic novels, films and heart-shaped merchandise,' I say, batting a dismissive hand.

The corner of her mouth twitches up. 'You reckon?'

'Yup.'

'Okay, well, thanks for that insight. It's really cheered me up.' Her ironic tone is laced with amusement.

It takes me right back to when we were dating. I'd found her dry sarcasm a real turn-on when we'd first got together – or, I should say, when we first started fucking.

She seems to think she's crossed a line of politeness though because she takes a step back and flips me an apologetic smile. 'Anyway, I think it's probably time I checked in and went straight to bed. I barely slept at all on the flight.'

As much as I don't want them to, my thoughts immediately turn to an image of her naked, climbing into her bed.

What the fuck is wrong with me? Is horniness a side effect of jetlag? Maybe it's because my body's aware it's unlikely to get any action in the immediate future and is rebelling.

Well, it can rebel all it likes, there's no way on earth Chloe and I will be partaking in any kind of skin-on-skin activity. She's clearly hurting from her relationship falling apart and I'm guessing she probably wants nothing to do with men right now.

'Okay. Well, have a good holiday. It's good to see you. A mind-fuck, but a cool one,' I say, stepping aside so she can get to the reception desk.

I nod to the receptionist, who hands me back my passport and a room key, and I turn to leave.

'Yeah, fucked up, but good to see you too,' Chloe says, giving me a tight smile, then turning away to check in at the desk.

I feel well and truly dismissed.

Which is fine by me. I just want to get to my room and chill for a while now anyway.

A porter appears as if by magic and gives me a polite bow before picking up my case and leading me away from the desk and towards the apartment where I'm going to be staying. It's one of five exclusive residences dotted along the riverbank and is nestled amongst the lush greenery of the hotel's extensive grounds. They have both tennis and paddle courts at the far end as well as a whole separate building housing a spa where they offer the most cutting-edge treatments available.

The rich and famous often book in here specifically to use the world-class facilities and re-energise after a heavy work stint.

Tiredness swamps me and I let out a big yawn as I follow him through a beautifully curated Japanese-style garden, with its waterfall running gently into a pond full of koi fish.

Perhaps a power nap will sort me out. Reset my body-clock. Then I'll be ready to get into my holiday.

I glance back towards the main building of the hotel.

I wonder if that's the last I'll see of Chloe Dasher?

2

CHLOE

Jeez, that was awkward.

Of all the times to bump into Kit!

If you'd asked me to guess when I'd have been most likely to see him again, my honeymoon-for-one in Japan would *not* have featured on the list.

I actually feel a bit shaky from the shock of seeing him again.

How bizarre that he's here after his own failed wedding too.

As I'd stared into his handsome, spine-tinglingly familiar face, after he'd asked me what I was doing here, I'd felt a strong urge to make something up about being on a scouting mission for my job or something, but at the very last second I decided *what's the point?* I'd only have to keep up the ruse all week during the numerous times I'm bound to bump into him, since we're both staying here.

I'm way too stressed already to put up with that kind of bullshit.

And I've never been the type to mince my words, as my friends and my ex will tell you.

As Kit will tell you too.

My skin heats as I remember the hot sex we used to have all those years ago. Unfortunately, it had become obvious pretty quickly that there was no future for us as a couple – he had no interest in getting into anything serious, which I'd wanted from a relationship at the time – so it had been better for us to finish things and move on.

He'd not seemed too cut up about it, but I'd had a few moments of regret right after we'd split when I wondered whether I'd done the right thing.

But then I got together with Adrian and barely saw Kit around after that, and he'd mostly faded into the background of my life.

I'm sure he wasn't on his own for long either. He was always really popular.

And even if getting married didn't work out for him this time, I'm sure there will be plenty of gorgeous, willing women to take his ex's place the moment he's ready for them to sashay up to him.

Because he's a sexy guy.

And he can be funny.

And he's incredible in bed.

Hmm. Time to change the subject, I think, brain.

Kit Charleston is the very last person I should be thinking about right now. He wasn't right for me then and he's no doubt not right for me now. People don't change. Not really.

And I'm probably only projecting these inappropriate feelings onto him because of how out of control Adrian's left me feeling.

Sexual jealousy is a potent aphrodisiac.

I take my passport back from the receptionist when she

hands it over and return her bow as she gives me the key card to my room.

'The porter will be back any moment to take your suitcase to your room and show you around, madam,' the receptionist says.

I hold up my hand. 'No need. Thank you. Can you just point me in the right direction? I'd rather find my room myself. And I'm fine with my suitcase,' I add. I really don't want to get into the whole *do I tip?* head-mash thing again.

'Of course,' the receptionist says with a confused smile. Clearly people who come here don't normally tend to lug their own bags around. 'You're down this corridor, to the very end, and it's the last room on the right.'

'Thanks,' I say, giving her a bright smile, before setting off in the direction she's sent me.

I find my room easily and let myself in with the key card.

After taking off my shoes in the entrance hall and pointing them towards the door, I walk into the room and gasp in glee. It's even more beautiful than the website made it look. I'd been worried it would actually be a bit pokey and more soulless than it seemed in the pictures, but no. It's perfect.

There's a huge black-lacquered four-poster bed, with crisp white cotton sheets and squidgy-looking pillows, and on each side hang semi-opaque silk drapes which can be pulled round for privacy. By both sides of the bed stand elegant urushi-e black-lacquered cabinets with paper panels and gold detail handles. The walls of the room are painted in a soft duck-egg blue and there's wood-coloured rush matting on the floor, giving the sense of the outdoors inside. Through the large windows I can see the lush green banks of the river and the water flowing past, the sun glinting off the surface and making it sparkle.

It's the height of opulence and good taste.

Leaving my suitcase by the wardrobe, I stumble over to the

bed, pull off my clothes, which I leave in an untidy pile on the floor, and crawl under the covers.

I'm so ridiculously tired now after being up for a whole day there's no way I'm keeping my eyes open till 9 p.m., like they advise you do if your flight lands in the morning.

Sod that. I need to sleep. Just for a couple of hours. Then I'll be refreshed and ready to enjoy my first evening here.

My eyelids are so heavy now I have to squint through them to set the alarm on my phone, and once that's done I dump it onto the nightstand and pull the covers up over my head, immediately sinking into a beautiful deep sleep.

Kit

I can't sleep.

Even though my body's telling me it's actually the early hours of the morning in the UK and I should have a kip, my brain is determined to keep me awake.

Bloody Chloe Dasher.

Seeing her has made my mind spin and dredged up intense memories of how hot we'd been together.

She's still got it. More than *it* in fact.

I can't help but laugh, though not with any kind of joy.

Bloody hell.

Talk about bad timing.

Why did I have to bump into her now, when she's in a bad place?

And how did my life go tits-up like this?

It was looking so good there for a while. I had everything I'd ever wanted. Money, status, a beautiful fiancée, excitement about my future. The world was my fucking oyster.

So how did I end up here? Alone in Kyoto? Like some shit homage to a noughties pop song.

Although, to be fair I'm not entirely alone. Not if I don't want to be.

I had thought, before I came here, that that's what I needed, but actually now I'm on the ground and I've had a moment to come round, I'm beginning to wonder whether I'll go a bit stir-crazy on my own.

Maybe I should go for a swim in the communal hotel pool and see who's around. Check the place out a bit. There might be other people like me that I can strike up a conversation with to distract myself. In fact there are bound to be. There might even be someone I recognise here.

Someone else.

I'm not expecting, or hoping, to see Chloe there though. I suspect she'll be dead to the world right now, judging by how tired she'd said she was.

Yeah. A swim and a drink by the pool might be just the thing to calm my rattled nerves.

I take a fast shower and change into my swimwear, then put on the robe and sliders the hotel has helpfully left by the door.

The path to the outdoor pool is quiet, but when I reach the poolside it's buzzing with people. There are a couple of loungers free on the opposite side of the pool, so I head over to them and lay my towel along one.

I'll take a swim first, before lying on it. It's pretty warm here, even though we're still in the spring season. It's certainly much warmer than it was when I left the UK anyway.

I prepare to dive in at the deep end, aware of a small group of women lounging in the water at the shallow end of the pool, sipping cocktails. I feel their gazes on me, and the attention gives me a thrill.

Yeah, I've still got it. Even if Katya doesn't want me any more, there'll be plenty of women who do. I know my strengths and make the most of them. I've had to. She's been working as a model for the last year and was always surrounded by the hippest, most attractive people, so I've been taking good care of myself. It's taken me hours a day in the gym and an eye-watering fee employing the skills of one of the top personal stylists in London to create the appearance I'm rocking now. Tough work, but totally worth it.

It turns out even a perfectly honed body and thousand-pound personally tailored suits weren't enough to keep Katya's attention though.

She's now back with her ex, I hear, even though it's only been a month since she killed our engagement. He's a billionaire too and Raffa tells me he's recently bought the coolest, most exclusive fashion house of the moment, which, surprise-surprise, she's going to be the new face of. A hot ticket to ultra-fame, for a model.

So that explains a lot.

One of Katya's skills is getting friendly with people who are going to get her to where she wants to go. Fame and success are her key driving forces, which didn't used to bother me when we first got together – I'm ambitious too – but this swerve back to her ex smacks of desperation for the limelight.

Which is *not* attractive.

Anyway, I'm not going to think on that shit while I'm here.

I take a step to the edge of the pool and launch myself in.

I'm pleased with how smooth the dive is, and I power through the water, enjoying the cooling effect against my skin. When I get to the shallow end, I pause for a second to nod to the women, who all smile back at me, flashing startlingly white teeth, before setting off on my next lap.

Yeah, this is going to be good for me.

Restore my faith in myself.

I do twenty laps of the pool before I feel tiredness dragging at me. Time to get out and lie in the sun for a while. Top up my tan.

As I'm walking back to my lounger, I signal for the waiter to come over and take my drink order, a bottle of Japanese lager, then stretch out, feeling the sun start to warm my cool, wet skin.

This is the life.

My drink arrives quickly and I chug most of it in one go, surprised by how thirsty I am. I guess that's the dehydrating effect of flying for you.

There's a gentle sound of happy conversation and tinkling laughter coming from the other side of the pool, but I don't look over at the women again. I'm too tired to engage in any more eye-fucking right now.

Instead, I close my eyes and let the alcohol and the waves of heat on my skin soothe me into a blissful sleep.

3

CHLOE

My alarm wakes me up with a start. I'm disorientated for a few seconds and can't work out where I am.

Then it all comes flooding back to me.

I'm in Japan. On my honeymoon. Without the key ingredient: a husband.

And Kit is here.

Rolling onto my back, I stare up at the ceiling. My skin feels tingly and strange, like someone's just gently caressed me with their fingertips and all my nerve endings have sprung to attention.

It must be the jetlag.

I roll over and sit up, giving myself a shake. Time to wake up and get out and about, otherwise I'll never sleep tonight and my body-clock will be out of sync for the rest of my time here. If I was able to afford to stay for two weeks it wouldn't have mattered so much, but I can't, so I'm going to need to be organised about getting the most out of my time.

Maybe a swim will freshen me up.

I find my tankini and pull a vest top and shorts on over the top of it. I'm not sure if it's okay to take the towel from my room, but I figure since I'm paying five-star prices, the least they can do is provide me with an extra towel when I need one. I'll ask reception about getting one later. I drop my phone, sunglasses and the paperback I was reading on the plane into the tote I've brought, in case I feel like hanging out by the pool once I've had a swim.

It's quiet inside the hotel and I don't see anyone else as I stroll down the corridor, following the signs towards the outdoor pool. It becomes clear why it's so deserted when I walk out into the pool area and find it thronged with people. If fact there's only one lounger available.

And it's next to the one person I hoped I wouldn't see out here.

Kit seems to be asleep, stretched out in the sunshine, his body gleaming in the light like some golden trophy. He's looking good. Really good. Clearly he's been working out at the gym a lot as he's more ripped than I remember him being when I first knew him – not that he wasn't always fit.

But this vision in front of me is something else entirely.

My body floods with heat, and desire starts to coil through me.

Dammit.

This is the last thing I need.

I'm in mourning for my last relationship and I don't need the complication of my inappropriate age-old lust for Kit to add to my torment.

It's nice to know my libido hasn't completely died though. That there's still some life in the old girl.

Anyway, sod this. I'm not going to spend my time here hiding in my room. I have just as much right to be by this poolside as he does. It's not like I'm stalking him. It's just pure coincidence that the only space available is right next to him.

So I stride over and dump my bag next to the free lounger, then spread my towel out along the cushion, keeping my gaze determinedly off Kit's sleeping form. Turning my back on him – just in case he wakes up and thinks I'm deliberately stripping in front of him – I pull off my vest and shorts and drop them on top of the towel before walking over to the other side of the pool and tentatively dipping my toe into the water.

It's just the right temperature, warm enough not to give me a heart attack when I get into it but cool enough to not make me hot while I swim.

I do a few lengths of breaststroke, keeping my gaze fixed in front of me and not allowing myself to glance over to where Kit is still asleep on the lounger.

At least I assume he's still asleep. For all I know he could be watching me right now, with his dark-eyed gaze assessing my performance.

He's got the most incredible eyes. They're the deepest brown I've ever seen and can look almost black in some situations. Whenever he'd look at me, back in the day, with his intense gaze, my whole body would feel fizzy with lust.

It was like he was sexing me with his eyes. I know that sounds weird, but he just has a way of turning me on with his attentiveness.

Had a way.

I'm not falling for that surface-level kind of attention again. Because that's what I realised it was. He never took our relationship seriously. He was the kind of guy who was always on the lookout for the next new thing. Or that's what it felt like, anyway.

It sounds like he found a person he was happy to stick with

though, if he was going to get married. Katya, I think he called her. I imagine she's just as attractive and cool as he is. Those things always seemed to really matter to him.

I finally allow myself to glance in his direction and my heart starts to race when I see that he's awake and is in fact watching me.

How is it possible to actually feel someone's gaze on you? It's like he's physically touching me right now, judging by how my body's reacting.

Dammit.

Well, he'll soon get bored with it. With me. No doubt. There are a lot of beautiful women here at the hotel, sitting around the pool in their tiny designer bikinis, their long, toned and tanned limbs stretched out in perfectly poised poses.

And I'm not here to flirt with Kit. I've come to have a relaxing, restorative time.

With that affirmation in mind, I climb out of the pool and walk, dripping, over to my lounger.

'Looking strong there, Dasher,' Kit says as I move my clothes so I can pick up my towel and pat myself dry with it before laying it back onto the lounger.

'Thanks,' I say, keeping my tone friendly, but final. I don't want to get into a conversation with him about the state of our bodies.

No way am I admitting out loud that I've even noticed what his body looks like.

'Do you still dance?' he asks, clearly undeterred by my indifferent tone.

'Whenever I can,' I say, sitting on the lounger and making myself comfortable. Taking my sunglasses out of the tote, I put them on and lie back, hoping he'll take the hint that I don't really want to chat right now.

He doesn't.

'You always did love to dance. I remember you doing it for hours whenever we went out clubbing.'

'Hmm.'

'I've not been to a club for a while. Katya, my ex, didn't like dancing.'

'Oh. Shame.'

There's silence for about thirty seconds before he says, 'So what else do you do with your time now?'

I let out a jokey sort of sigh then turn to look at him.

Which is a mistake.

He's looking back at me in that intent way of his and I feel something dangerous stir deep inside me. It's that pull of desire I always felt whenever he was around. It's what attracted me to him in the first place and what kept us together for as long as it did over those few intensely sexually charged months.

I look away quickly and try to compose myself before speaking. I'm terrified my voice is going to come out wobbly.

'Um... I've been working for a charity that protects woodland and the endangered species that live in it since I graduated,' I say, relieved when it comes out sounding relatively normal.

'Oh wow,' he says, his deep voice infused with what sounds like real warmth. 'You must get a lot out of that.'

'I do,' I agree. 'It's a great place to work, but it's becoming increasingly difficult to get people to donate. Trees often get pushed down the pecking order when people are struggling to feed their kids. But they're such an important part of our ecosystem. And someone has to fight for them.'

'Thank God for people like you,' Kit says.

I think he genuinely means that too.

'Thanks,' I say, aware of heat rising up my neck to my face.

It's so weird sitting here with him, fielding his compliments.

The last time we'd been together for any significant amount of time we'd been awkwardly bringing our fling to an end. There hadn't been any real bad feeling between us, but we'd been pretty emotionally distant with each other.

'How about you?' I ask, aware I'm being rude by not asking him any questions back.

He bats a hand like it's of no consequence what he's been up to. 'Ah, you know. Business shit. I'm heavily investing in a new tech start-up which has the potential to be seriously disruptive. I can't talk much about it right now though. It needs time to incubate before we introduce it to the world, and we're trying to fly it under the radar of any competitors.'

He sits up and waves towards a guy on the other side of the pool, who's just finished serving drinks to a couple sitting on the loungers opposite us.

'Do you want a drink?' he asks me.

'Err... sure,' I say, caught off guard. I thought perhaps he was shutting down the conversation now, but it seems he's actually intent on keeping it going.

'I'll have a beer,' he says to the server when he gets to us, then looks at me with a questioning expression. 'And?'

I pause for a moment. Perhaps this isn't such a good idea. 'Actually, I'm fine.'

'You sure? It's on me. Go on, let me buy you a drink so we can raise a glass to our freedom.'

His smile is warm and friendly, and I have a sudden urge to stick one to Adrian by having a drink with my ex. An ex he hated. Plus I'm finding it very difficult to reject Kit's offer when he's being so charming.

'Okay. I'll have a cocktail,' I say wildly, feeling the need for something strong to help me relax. I'm a bit jangled, if I'm being honest, sitting here with him, trying to pretend this is a totally normal situation.

'Can you do me a Mai Tai?' I ask the server, scrambling for a cocktail I remember the name of. I know it's not a very Japanese drink, but my mind's gone completely blank.

'Yes, of course,' the server says, giving us both a nod before turning and heading over to the bar on the far side of the pool.

Kit doesn't comment on my choice of drink and lies back on his lounger and stares up at the sky.

Glad of a reprieve from his attention, I lie back too and close my eyes for a moment, enjoying the sensation of the sunshine on my face. It's been a while since I sunbathed, and it feels wonderful to be just lying here, not doing anything. I've been so busy at work and at the same time planning the wedding, I've not had much time to chill recently.

I try not to think about the money we've – or rather Adrian's – wasted on cancelling the wedding at the last minute. He promised he'd cover it and pay me back for any I've lost, since it's his fault we're in this horrible situation, but I'm still smarting about the time and energy I've wasted on it – and him.

Hot tears start to pool behind my eyes, and I have to force myself to think about something else so I don't start blubbing right here at the poolside in front of Kit. I really don't want him to feel like he has to look after me in any way.

Out of the corner of my eye I see him shift on his lounger, as if he's sensed I'm thinking about him, and I feel his gaze on me.

After a second I glance round at him, not wanting to seem impolite, but also not wanting to appear as if I'm up for a long, drawn-out chat right now.

'So how long are you here for?' he asks.

'Just a few days in Kyoto, but ten days in Japan,' I say.

He nods.

'You?' I ask.

'I'm planning on at least two weeks here at the hotel, but I'll see how I go.'

'At *least* two weeks?' I ask, a little incredulous. That amount of time must be costing him a fortune, but he's contemplating staying for *even longer*? He must have money to burn. I know his family is wealthy – he went to private school and they have a holiday home in France somewhere – but he never seemed to have a ton of money to spend when we were at uni and had a room in a basic, shared student flat, like the rest of us. I guess 'business' is good at the moment.

'It depends,' he says, shrugging. 'I might travel round Japan for a bit as well, but I'm not sure how much I'll want to do on my own.'

I just blink at him for a second as I live through a bizarre train of thought where the two of us end up travelling around together, exploring all the country has to offer.

Luckily I'm saved from having to make sense of that ridiculous diversion because the server returns with our drinks and puts them carefully onto the table between our two loungers.

'Thanks,' Kit says to him, and I smile and thank him as well.

We both pick up our respective drinks at the same time and Kit holds his out towards me. 'To freedom,' he says.

'To freedom,' I repeat, wishing I meant it.

We clink them together, then both take long sips before returning them to the table.

It's the weirdest thing, drinking a cocktail by the pool with Kit, instead of Adrian. Like I've accidentally tripped into a parallel universe or something.

'So how do you like your room here?' Kit asks me, propping his head on the heel of his hand and fixing me with his dark, hooded gaze.

Heat rushes up my spine.

'It's great. Actually, it's amazing. Exactly what I pictured and then some.'

He nods like he understands.

'How about your room? Is it what you expected?' I ask, wondering fleetingly whether we're next door to each other.

'Actually, I'm in one of the apartments. They're separate from the main part of the hotel so really private.'

I push my sunglasses down my nose and look at him over the top of them, then roll my eyes in mock jest. 'Of course you are. Only the best for you, right, Kit?' I say with a grin.

'What's wrong with wanting the best?' He sounds genuinely confused.

I shrug and quickly look away to watch the people who are swimming in the pool, before his penetrating gaze makes me wobble. 'It's fine for those who can afford it.'

'Well, you're staying at this hotel too, so I have to assume you're not exactly on the breadline yourself.'

I bristle. I really don't want to talk to him about my financial situation. 'I do okay,' I say, looking back at him. 'But I don't normally stay in five-star hotels. I've been saving for this one for ages because it's been on my bucket list to come here ever since I saw it on a TV show I love.'

'You mean that sexy one with all the couples having affairs with each other?' he asks, folding his arms and making the muscles bunch in his shoulders. I have to make a real effort to keep my gaze on his face.

'It had a bit more depth to the story than that,' I say, smiling. 'But yeah, I think we're talking about the same one. Did you like it?'

'Never saw it.'

'Really? I thought it'd be exactly your sort of thing,' I say, sitting up straighter in my lounger. I reach over to the table for my drink and take another big gulp of it.

'Oh yeah? Why's that?'

'Because of the inventive sex,' I say, feeling my skin buzz with a long-ignored yearning.

Our eyes lock and we stare at each other for a beat. I could swear the same thoughts about how inventive our sex had been are now also going through his mind.

'Jeez, I think this cocktail's gone straight to my head,' I say, aware of heat rushing up from my throat to my face again.

'Yeah. Drinking in the sun does that to me too. I lose all my inhibitions.' He flashes me a wolfish grin and I know for sure now that he was having the same thoughts as me.

There's another loaded pause where we just look at each other again. I swear his pupils have dilated and his eyes are now nearly entirely black.

A hot pulse of need beats between my thighs.

Oh, my God. I really need to move this conversation away from sex.

Maybe we should get back to the subject of money, that'll kill the mood. Clearly he has lots of it and he's bound to want to show off a little, in his arrogant, but charming, way.

Something suddenly occurs to me.

'Hang on a second. Don't the apartments have their own private swimming pools? I'm sure I saw that on the website,' I say.

There's a moment where he blinks at me and I get the impression he's trying to think of a good excuse for why he's not there right now. 'Yeah, I have a pool, but I thought I'd check out this one first. So I can give Elliot my feedback on the whole experience of being here.'

I frown, confused. 'Um... Sorry, I'm lost. Elliot? Your friend Elliot from uni?'

'The very same.'

'Why does he need feedback? Is he thinking about booking here for his own honeymoon?' I shift on my lounger so I can look at him more comfortably without cricking my neck. 'You might want to warn him there's a good chance this place is cursed for honeymooners, since the both of us have turned up here without a spouse.'

'It's his hotel,' he says, like I'm being a bit obtuse. 'Didn't you know?'

I sit up straighter. 'No. Since when?'

'Since he bought the whole Vanaheim Grand chain a couple of years ago.'

'He owns all the Vanaheim Grand hotels? How the *hell*? The last time I saw him he was eating pasta with ketchup because he'd run out of money for that month.'

Kit flashes me a grin. 'Yeah, well, he's come a long way since then. We all have.'

'Speak for yourself. I'm not sure coming "a long way" is how I'd describe my journey since uni. Don't get me wrong, I'm doing a job I like, but I have aspirations to go a lot further.'

There's a wry smile playing about his mouth now and I can tell he's about to tell me something else 'cool'. I can just sense it.

'Well, actually—' he begins.

I can't help but smile and shake my head in recognition at my insight.

He pauses and gives me a questioning frown.

'Sorry, please go ahead and tell me how brilliantly you're doing,' I say, loading my tone with jokey sarcasm.

'No, no. I wouldn't want to ruin your day any more than I already have,' he says, mirroring my mockery.

I'm suddenly keenly aware that this is the way we used to flirt with each other, and a memory of kissing him just to shut him up flies into my head. It had resulted in some of the best sex I've ever had.

My skin flushes with an electric sort of heat as flashes of that night come back to play through my mind.

What the *hell*? I'm supposed to be in mourning for my last relationship. I shouldn't be feeling like this, all hot and bothered and turned on.

It's bringing it home to me just how long it's been since I've felt that way though. Adrian never had this same effect on me, and the realisation is spinning me out a little.

'You know what? I think I'm going to go back to my room and chill there for a bit before dinner,' I blurt, reaching with a shaky hand for my tote bag.

He frowns. 'Hey, wait. Don't let me chase you off.'

'You're not. I'm just a bit wired for company right now.' I stand up and pull on my shorts and vest, then pick up my towel from the lounger and shove it into the tote.

'Okay. Well, it was good chatting,' he says, watching me with a slightly bemused expression.

'It was,' I say, flashing him a tight grin.

I really need to get out of here now.

Picking up my cocktail, I drain the last of it, then return the glass to the table. 'Thanks for the drink.'

'Welcome.'

'See you around,' I say.

'Not if I see you first.' I look back at him and catch him cringing a little at his words. 'Yeah, okay, that was lame.'

I can't stop the grin that pushes at the corners of my mouth. He always could make me smile, even when I was trying not to.

But I really should go.

No good can come of being around Kit Charleston.

4

KIT

I'm a bit surprised – and disappointed – that Chloe got up and left so abruptly.

I'd thought we'd been getting on pretty well, but it seems I rubbed her the wrong way somehow.

We'd always ribbed each other in the past – it was our way – but she appears to be averse to jokey banter today.

She seemed pretty flat too, like she's lost her spark.

But then I guess that's not surprising considering what's happened to her recently.

I look around me at the other guests who are still enjoying the lit vibes of the ambient techno music, on-trend cocktails and happy chatter around the pool, but being here doesn't hold the same allure now I'm alone again. So I decide to pack up and go back to my apartment too.

On the way there I stop at reception to chat to them about my dinner plans. I asked my PA to email and let them know I wanted to eat in my private dining room, at least for the first night, and I'm just going to check they got that information.

'Yes, sir,' the receptionist confirms. 'Your meal will be delivered to your apartment at seven o'clock, as you requested. Could I check, it's just a meal for one person, yes?'

Her question tugs at something deep inside me. I'm guessing Chloe's going to be eating on her own too.

'Actually, I'd like to eat in the restaurant instead. You'll have a table available for me, right?' I ask.

'Let me check, sir. We're very busy tonight, but I'm sure we can accommodate you,' the receptionist says with a smile.

I wait, tapping my fingers against my thighs, and glance around towards the bar while she does so. There's no-one in it at present as everyone seems to still be outside at the pool. I imagine it'll be jumping later though. I'll have to come and check it out.

'Yes, I can arrange a table for you,' she says, drawing my attention back to her.

I smile. 'Great. Book me in for seven o'clock then please.'

'I'll do that, sir,' she says, tapping on her keyboard.

'Thanks.' I give her a nod, then head back to my apartment.

Yeah, that's the right choice. I'll soak up the atmosphere in the restaurant tonight, then eat in my apartment for the next few days to get some proper peace.

I take a shower, then towel off and lie on my bed naked, staring up at the ceiling.

I'm feeling weirdly buzzed. Not sure why. I've gone away on my own before, on my year out before uni, so I'm used to travelling alone and making opportunities for fun as I go.

I'd come here thinking I needed some space, but that's not what I'm craving right now.

My body feels alive and primed.

And I seem to have a hard-on.

Maybe it's because I'm lying here naked.

It's funny because I've not felt like having sex since Katya took off, but my sex drive has suddenly returned with a vengeance.

Seeing Chloe has shaken me up. Taken me back to happier, more carefree times.

I genuinely thought I'd never see her again.

But I'm kinda glad I have.

It's spoken to something that's been buried in me. Reignited something, after feeling dead inside.

And consequently, I'm experiencing an irresistible drive to *do* something right now. I'm not entirely sure what, but I figure if I put myself out into the world, *something's* bound to happen.

I'm always up for an adventure.

I resist the urge to have a wank, wanting to preserve my energy for the time being, just in case I end up meeting someone tonight and hooking up with them is on the cards.

Instead, I waste some time messing about on the internet, then checking my accounts, taking great pleasure in the long strings of digits they all show.

Finally, my alarm goes off to let me know it's time to dress for dinner.

Rolling off the bed, I go over to my wardrobe where my clothes have been hung up by the personal butler I get with the apartment. He must have come in while I was out at the pool. I've asked for him to keep a low profile while I'm here and just come in when the place is empty unless I specifically ask for him. He seems to have done this, which I'm grateful for because I don't feel like making polite chitchat right now.

I get dressed in navy cargo pants and a fitted white T and style my hair, then spray on some aftershave. I've had one designed for me at great fucking expense, using the keynote fragrances I like, and it's a joy to wear. I love the idea that I don't smell like anyone else in the world.

I hear the hubbub of chatter coming from the dining room before I reach it and it suddenly hits me what I'm about to walk into. I brace myself for striding through the room alone to my table, hoping they've put me against a wall so I don't feel too exposed sitting there solo.

The greeter gives me a bow as I approach and says what I think is *hello and welcome* in Japanese. I give her my name and she checks it against a list on an e-tablet then beckons for me to follow her into the dining area.

It's a spectacular room of course, fitted out in the same kind of style as the reception, with the larger tables separated by free-standing square-patterned screens or hanging silk dividers. The sun is about to set, but through the floor-to-ceiling windows along the back wall I can still make out the wide river flowing below us in the dusky light.

I stride through the diners, chin up and chest out, trying to act as though I'm totally relaxed about eating in here on my own.

It'll be a good opportunity to do some people watching and check out who else is staying at the hotel, if nothing else, and I have my phone in my pocket, so I can sit and read something on that if it all gets a bit weird and uncomfortable. And I can always get my plate sent to my apartment and eat there after all if I get bored.

As I walk towards the only free table on the other side of the room that the greeter is heading for, I see with a shot of pleasure that I won't be the only person dining alone in here.

Chloe is watching me walk towards her with an expression on her face that very clearly says *Seriously?*

Her table set for one is slap bang next to *my* table set for one.

It's like the hotel have deliberately put us together.

Well, isn't that a funny coincidence.

'Before you say anything, I didn't orchestrate this. I swear,' I fib when I reach my table.

Apart from the bit where I changed where I was going to eat this evening – I *don't* admit.

'Uh huh.'

From the tone of her voice, she doesn't believe me.

I can't blame her. This must look exactly like the set-up it is.

Pulling out the chair, I sit down and nod my thanks to the greeter.

So this is fucking weird. We're sitting next to each other at separate tables, both looking out at the room and the empty space in front of us where our partners would have sat if they hadn't dumped us.

It's like we're being forced to face the stark reality of our singleness in the most exposing of ways.

It seems Chloe is feeling the same way because out of the corner of my eye I see her shift in her chair and uncross, then re-cross, her legs, then lift the menu from the table and pretend to study it, all the while politely ignoring my presence right next to her.

But I can *feel* her vibrating.

I know she's hyper aware of me right here next to her.

Because I'm vibrating too.

I give a jokey huff, shake my head then turn to face her. 'This is ridiculous. Why don't we just share a table tonight if we're both eating on our own?'

She turns and looks at me with an expression of resigned capitulation on her face. 'It was inevitable, I suppose, that we'd be shoved next to each other since we appear to be the only single people staying at the hotel.'

'Glad to hear you're so happy about the idea of spending more time with me,' I say drolly.

She sighs. 'It's not that. It's just – I was expecting to spend my time here getting used to my own company again. I thought it would be good for me to prove to myself I could do it – have a good time, that is – without relying on anyone else to prop me up.'

'We could just sit and not talk if you like?' I say. 'Or not.' I shrug, keeping my tone nonchalant. 'Whatever. I'm happy to sit on my own if you don't want company right now.'

There's a pause where she stares down at her menu again, her brow furrowed, before turning back and giving me a tight smile.

'Yeah, maybe you're right. It'd be a lot less weird. I feel like everyone's staring at us both sitting here side by side like a couple of losers. Are you sure I'm not cramping your style?'

I let out an exasperated laugh. 'Jesus Christ, Dasher, just move your arse over here to my table and stop overthinking it, will you?'

She blinks at me, then gives me a reluctant grin and shakes her head. 'You haven't changed.'

'Actually, I think you'll find I have. In all the best ways,' I say, pushing out the chair opposite me with my foot as she gets up from her table and relocates to mine.

Sitting down, she shifts her chair in closer, then looks straight back down at her menu, pointedly avoiding my gaze.

So I pick up my own menu and study it.

All the meals look amazing, but I'm suddenly a lot less hungry than I was before I sat down. Even so, I pick something that looks like it might not be too filling and select which sake I'd like so I'm ready when the waiting staff comes over to take our order. Chloe puts in her order too, also choosing to drink sake, and the server takes our menus away, leaving Chloe with nothing to distract her, so she's forced to look at me.

'Food options look good,' I say, to break the awkward atmosphere.

'Yeah. They do,' she agrees. 'There's a lot more fish and seafood than I was expecting though.'

'You're not a fan?'

'I am. I just don't cook it much, so don't tend to eat it. But I told myself before I came here that I'd expand my menu choices and not just go for the sorts of dishes I'd usually pick.'

'Good idea. I guarantee you the food here will be spectacular, no matter what you pick.'

'I'm sure.'

'Elliot's very hot on his restaurants competing with the best cuisine available around the world.'

Her eyebrows raise in polite question. 'So you're obviously still in contact with Elliot then? And Raffa too?'

I nod. 'Yeah. We speak a lot, even though we're all involved in other lines of work now.'

She leans in a little closer. 'Other lines? Did you end up working together then?'

'Yeah. You remember we were all on the same business degree course? Well, Elliot's a shit-hot programmer as well – quite the lucrative hobby – and after we'd graduated, we all formed a company and launched an app that he'd been developing in his spare time. Raffa took on the CEO role and I funded all the marketing and promotion with money my grandpa left me when he died. It went gangbusters. People fell on it for a new way to create content for social media and news reporting. Right place, right time etcetera. We got lucky with two rival tech giants really wanting it when we decided to sell, which meant it went to a bidding war which neither of them wanted to lose, so we got a higher than the anticipated price for it. A lot higher.'

Her eyes are wide now. 'Oh my God, that was you guys? I saw something on the news about the crazy price that an app developed by a UK-based company sold for, but I didn't realise you were in involved in it.' She bestows me with a nod of respect. 'Well done.'

'Thanks. We were pleased.'

'I bet.'

Our glasses of sake arrive and she raises hers in a congratulatory manner.

I lift mine and clink it against hers, then take a sip. It tastes amazing. In fact my taste buds seem to have come properly alive again now.

'So what? You're all millionaires now?' she asks, putting her drink down again.

'Actually, we're all billionaires.'

'Oh my God.' She lets out a strangled-sounding laugh. 'This is like a wet dream come true for you, isn't it?'

I lean back in my chair and put my hands behind my head, stretching my crooked arms in a jokey peacocking motion. 'I bet you're wishing you hadn't left me now, huh?'

She rolls her eyes at me, but follows it with an amused grin. 'When you say arrogant shit like that it makes me remember exactly why I *did* break up with you,' she says, though her voice is light with humour.

'I'm just kidding around,' I reassure her.

'Yeah, I know. Though honestly, back then I didn't care how much money you had. I liked you because you made me laugh and we had chemistry.'

I release my pose and sit forwards in my chair, locking my gaze with hers. 'And I'm smoking in bed.'

'Jesus.' She closes her eyes, her lips fighting another smile. 'What?'

Opening them again, she looks straight at me. 'You're so damn performative. You always were.'

'What do you mean?'

'It's like you're trying to prove something all the time. Why do you do that? No-one here's judging you, especially not me.'

I blink at her, bristling at her words. 'Still not pulling your punches I see.'

She shrugs. 'I don't need to with you. I feel like I can be totally honest without worrying about pissing you off because you know and understand me. And anyway, I'm not in the mood for boosting men's egos right now, I'm afraid. Feel free to get up and leave if you like. I'm very happy to be on my own if I'm not the sort of company you're after right now. I'd totally understand.'

'Okay, okay, point taken. Maybe I was being a bit of a dick there,' I say, holding up my hands in surrender and moderating my tone to light-hearted ribbing. 'No more posturing, I promise.' I chase this statement with a grin.

She rubs a hand over her eyes. 'Look, sorry if I'm coming across as a bit abrasive,' she says with passion in her voice, 'but I've come to realise recently, after what happened with Adrian, that it doesn't pay to be nice all the time. Be a good person, sure – a kind person when it's called for – but being *nice* means you get walked over and left behind. I'm not prepared to have that happen to me again. So I'm setting boundaries and sticking to them and being honest about what I need in order to be happy – as happy as I can be.' She points at her chest. 'I'm taking care of me now.'

Her gaze drops from mine and she reaches for her sake again, taking another long sip of it.

There's a weird sort of tension hanging in the air between us now that I'm not sure how to break.

Maybe this was a bad idea, sitting together.

She continues to stare down at the table, blinking rapidly, and it suddenly hits me that she's trying to hold back tears.

'Are you okay?' I ask gently.

'I just feel so stupid,' she says, so quietly I barely hear it.

'Stupid? Why?'

'Because I didn't see it. With Adrian. It was there, right under my nose. So obvious, now I think about it.'

'I hope you're not blaming yourself,' I say hotly. 'He's the stupid dickhead for cheating on you.'

She nods, but still doesn't look up at me.

'Seriously, Dasher. The guy's an absolute tool for treating you like that.'

'Can we change the subject?' she says. Her voice sounds strangled, like she's still trying to stop the tears.

'Yeah, sure. Of course.' I fold my arms and sit back in my chair. 'Tell me about what you're planning to do while you're here in Kyoto.'

I watch as she shuffles in her seat, gives a little cough then sits up straighter, pushing her shoulders back and finally lifting her chin to look at me and give another tight smile. Her eyes are a little bloodshot, and a mixture of empathy for her pain and anger at her twat-of-an-ex for making her feel like that threads through me.

She deserves better than to be treated like that.

We both deserve better.

Especially from the people who we thought loved us.

Not seeming to notice my internal turmoil, she launches into outlining her plans for while she's staying here.

'So, I'm going to take one of the boat trips down the river

here. And go to the bamboo forest at dawn, when apparently the light looks beautiful through the canes. And I want to go into the city and look around, get a feel of the place. Oh, and I *have* to visit a cat café while I'm here of course. I've never been to one and I hear they're really fun.'

I make a face. 'Cats? Really? I didn't know you were into cats.'

'Yeah. What's wrong with liking cats?'

'Nothing.'

'Apparently they often have kittens to play with too.'

I grin-grimace. 'Cute.'

She doesn't rise to my teasing.

'And on completely the other end of the scale, I've booked myself in for Samurai training a couple of days from now.'

'Whoa. Hold up. Samurai training?'

'Yeah. They do it at a dojo in the middle of Kyoto. You get to wield a real sword at the end to cut through some bamboo or something. It looks like a lot of fun.'

'That does sound fun,' I admit. I quite fancy doing that myself.

'How about you? What have you got planned?' she asks, picking up her sake and draining the last of it from the glass.

'Um... well, I'll probably do a boat trip too and maybe visit some shrines and temples,' I hedge. I don't want to look like a boring bastard and admit I've not planned anything concrete to do with my time yet.

'Ooh, yes,' she says, her eyes lighting up. 'I'd like to visit some of the temples too. There are a few other things I'd love to do if I can squeeze them in as well.'

I watch her talk as she lists her other plans for her trip in between mouthfuls of the food that's arrived while we've been talking, marvelling at how effortlessly cool she is, how inspiring and proactive.

Katya never planned anything for us to do together, she always left it up to me to arrange things to do to entertain us. And she was a tough crowd to please. She expected the best of everything. Exclusivity. No expense spared.

Chloe seems to be the opposite. Full of life and fire, proactive and interested in everything.

I dig that.

My brain seems to be suddenly buzzing with the dopamine hits I'm getting off sitting here with her, listening to her talk in that animated way she has.

Which is wild.

The last thing I'd expected, when I decided to come here to get some space from my failed relationship with Katya, was to end up having cravings for an ex from years ago instead.

But Chloe's presence here has lit a fire inside me.

I think her resolve to have a good time, despite being emotionally bulldozed, is inspiring.

It's suddenly really important that she can see that I've changed.

And I want her to enjoy herself while she's here – hopefully in my company.

She puts her chopsticks down onto her now cleared plate and gives me a satisfied smile.

'Want to come back to my apartment for a night swim?' I ask her.

5

CHLOE

I'm not sure why I said yes to this – something to do with the sake, I'm sure – but here I am, in Kit's private pool, in my tankini, clinging to the side with my second, now mostly empty, glass of rice wine in my hand, while I watch him swim lengths.

The bar in his apartment appeared to be stocked with every high-end branded spirit available, but I'd refused a cocktail – which, apparently, he could have called on his *butler* to come over and make for me – and opted instead to stick with what I've already been drinking. The last thing I want is to take out a day of my holiday by suffering with a hangover.

He stops at the far end of the pool and looks back towards me, raising one eyebrow in a questioning manner, checking I'm okay.

I smile and give him a thumbs up.

He seems satisfied with this and dives under the water again, powering his lithe body back towards me.

It's not the most *terrible* night I've ever had. Not even close.

In fact, as I watch him swim, I feel for a moment as if I've entered one of my fantasies – one of the ridiculous unlikely-to-ever-happen ones.

Yet, here I am. Living it.

I keep asking myself what the hell I think I'm doing, but the answer I keep coming back to is: I'm just having a bit of fun. Don't I deserve it after the crap I've been through recently? And Kit is nothing if not fun. He always was.

He's not the kind of guy you get serious with though.

I don't think he's got the staying power I'd need from a partner. He certainly didn't back when we knew each other before. And I'm guessing that's the conclusion his ex-fiancée came to as well.

As if he's sensed I'm thinking about him, he stops swimming when he reaches my end of the pool, then wades over to me, smoothing the water droplets from his face, then running his fingers through his thick dark hair, slicking it back against his head. I watch in fascination as the muscles in his chest move beneath his skin.

There's a fluttering sensation deep in my stomach and unfortunately, I don't think it's the booze that's causing it.

'This is the life, right?' he says, flipping me a grin.

'Yes. It is,' I reply stiffly, forming my mouth into a wide smile. I'm still not entirely sure about the wisdom of being here with him right now.

He must sense my reticence because he cocks his head and fixes me with that dark, penetrating gaze of his.

The fluttering intensifies.

'Come on, Dasher, do a few lengths with me. It'll help with the frustration.' He waggles his eyebrows at me.

I can't help but laugh at that, but I wave a dismissive hand in the air at his suggestion. 'Nah. I don't feel like swimming again right now.'

'No?'

'No.'

His gaze is still steady on me, as if he's trying to penetrate my mind.

Then he lets out a loud sigh and moves to lean against the side next to me, turning to catch my eye again.

The heat of his body radiates towards me, and I catch the scent of his aftershave in the air. It's delicious and intoxicating – an alluring blend of musky undertones – and it makes my head swim in an extremely pleasurable way.

'Look, *fuck* Adrian and *fuck* Katya,' he says in his low, seductive voice. 'They're the losers. Because they're not here, swimming in the moonlight in Kyoto right now – but we are.' His gaze is intent on mine and when he smiles at me, I can't help but stare at his sensual, full mouth and remember how much I used to love kissing him. And how much I enjoyed the feel of his mouth on me. Everywhere.

I give an involuntary full-body shiver, which starts at the base of my spine and rushes outwards, to caress the whole of my skin.

Kit frowns. 'You cold? Want to warm up in the hot tub?' he asks.

'Err, yeah, sure,' I say. Though I'm not sure it's a great idea to be putting myself in even closer proximity to him right now.

I don't go back on my decision though, determined not to be a killjoy, and I follow him as he gets out of the pool and heads over to the sunken hot tub on the other side of his private terrace, that no doubt has amazing views across the river in the daylight.

At night though, we're faced with a deep navy darkness, with only pinpricks of light in the distance from the lights of the nearest town.

Luckily, the moon is bright tonight and is giving off just enough light for us to see what we're doing without it feeling like we've got a spotlight trained on us.

Kit steps down into the tub first and moves over to the far side so I can follow him in. As soon as he's settled, I climb in directly opposite him, as far away from temptation as I can get.

We sit quietly for a few moments, both luxuriating in the feel of the hot bubbling water on our skin, which is intense after the cool pool.

'How are you doing now, Dash?' he asks me, raising a quizzical eyebrow.

I can't help but smile at his friendly concern.

'Ah, you know. I'm trying to stay positive, in amongst all this luxury.'

He smiles back at me. 'Yeah. It's the only way to be. Life moves fast and there's no point in clinging on to something you have no power to change. It'll only slow you down.'

'Are you trying to tell me not to have any regrets?'

'I guess so, yeah.'

'If only it were *that* easy to trick my brain into believing everything's okay.'

'We can only try.'

'Yeah. We can,' I agree.

Kit leans back against the side of the tub and stretches his arms out in front of him. 'So in the spirit of positive thinking, what are you looking for in your next partner?' he asks me, swishing his hands through the water in front of him.

I clear my throat and sit up straighter, energised by his question. This is something I've put a lot of thought into over the last few days in an attempt to keep myself from totally falling apart.

I'm determined to think about this as an opportunity for

change, just as Sadie suggested, instead of the loss of everything I once knew.

'Someone who's honest and respectful,' I say, propping my head against the padded headrest behind me and looking up at the night sky. 'Who looks out for people, but does it subtly and doesn't look for recognition and gratitude all the bloody time. Adrian was a bit of a pain in the arse like that. I always felt like he was stepping up so he could prove how manly he was, so people would give him the credit he thought he deserved. I'd like to be with someone who's humble, but intrinsically knows his own worth and spends his time meaningfully. He's got to be self-assured, but also be able to let other people take the lead and be in control. And he'll support me and do his share of the hard, boring and icky things that need to be done, but he won't bitch about it, just get on with it. So I guess I want him to have integrity and show up consistently, even when things are hard. And he should push himself to be the best person he can be. But most of all, I want to be with someone who's kind. That's really important to me.'

He's staring at me like I've just blown his mind.

'Jesus. You don't want much, do you?' he jokes, but there's a definite undertone of incredulity in his tone.

'Good job I'm not asking it of you then,' I shoot back.

There's a heavy silence where we blink at each other.

Dammit. I shouldn't have said that. It was way past the point of being an okay thing to say, in fact.

'Look, sorry. I – err, I think I'm a bit too emotionally messed up for this kind of conversation. I didn't mean to take it in that direction. I'm still really upset about what Adrian did to me and you're getting the brunt of my frustration instead of him.' I hold up my hands, the water running down them in rivulets. 'I apologise. I'm normally better than I used to be at not being so blunt with people, but I guess I'm not masking it so well with you tonight.' I screw up my nose in an expression of regret. 'You should take it as a compliment. It means I'm comfortable enough with you to show you the real me.'

Kit frowns. 'It sounds like you have some serious anger issues to deal with,' he says, his voice loaded with what feels like judgement.

Irritation flashes through me, turning my face hot. 'Can you blame me? I was literally jilted at the alter on the day of my wedding. It doesn't get much more humiliating than that. And I can't take it out on the person who I'm really angry with because he's not here. He's off being happy, fucking someone else.'

'Yeah, I get that, but I'm not here to be your emotional punch bag, Dasher. I want to have a good time and forget about my own shit. Because believe it or not I have issues to deal with too.'

Shame floods through me. He's right; I'm being a selfish bitch, harping on about my woes when he's been kind enough to invite me here to hang out with him. I guess I've been thinking about him like he used to be, back in our uni days, when he seemed so carefree and unencumbered by any kind of angst. But he's had his fair share of emotional upset too recently.

'Sorry,' I say, 'I shouldn't be taking it out on you, it's totally unfair of me to do that.'

'Thanks for the apology.'

'You're welcome.'

There's another loaded pause where we both adjust our seating position and pretend to be fascinated by the movement of the water in front of us.

'Perhaps you could find another way to channel your anger?' Kit says after a few moments of quiet.

'Yeah? Like how?'

Kit shrugs and looks away, but I can tell from the way he's keeping his lips clamped shut that he definitely has a suggestion, but isn't sure he should share it with me.

It seems we've both put our walls up.

I want to get back to the flirty banter we were engaged in earlier, but I'm not sure how to do it.

'Jesus, what just happened here?' I blurt, throwing my hands up and showering water droplets into the air in front of me. 'It was all going so well.'

'Was it?' His eyebrow is raised in amused derision now.

Which is fair enough.

'No. I guess not,' I say.

He flashes me a smile, which I can't help but return.

He's such a charismatic guy. It's impossible not to be charmed by him.

'Why do you think it didn't work out with your ex?' I ask, throwing the focus back onto him to give me a chance to get a handle on my see-sawing emotions.

He sits back in the tub, with his arms stretched out on either side of him along the rim, displaying the toned muscles in his arms to great effect. His brow is furrowed and he's staring into the bubbling water as if he's seriously considering my question.

After a moment of silence, where I wonder if I've gone too far in asking him about this right now, he finally looks at me again, his expression turning rueful.

'She's easily distracted and her ex snuck in under the radar and tempted her back. I guess she was partly with me because of the money and status I provided, and he came along offering her more. We had a blast when we first got together, but we weren't seeing much of each other by the end because she was always away working. We'd started to drift.'

'So why did you want to marry her?'

He blows out a long, low sigh and stares into the tub again. 'I loved her. She's a really cool, funny person. Exciting to be around when she *was* around. And I guess I thought it might cement our relationship and ground me or something. I've been feeling a bit untethered after offloading the app. So much of my self-worth and status was wrapped up in building then selling the business.'

I blink at him, trying to process what he's telling me.

'How did you think she was going to help with that "untetheredness" if she was away all the time?' I ask, as gently as I can.

Clearly it doesn't come out as tactfully as I'd intended because he lets out a snort and shakes his head in bemusement. 'I don't know. I guess I was more focused on how good she made me feel about myself when we were together.'

'Because she's cool and exciting and beautiful and she chose you?'

He looks up and catches my eye. 'You really *haven't* lost that bluntness, have you?'

I shrug awkwardly in apology.

He waves a dismissive hand in the air. 'Look, can we talk about something else? We've split up now so there's no point in dissecting it.'

'Sure.' I show my palms in surrender. 'I just thought it might help you make a better choice for your next partner if you knew why this one didn't work out.'

'Thanks, but I don't need your help in analysing my bad decisions. I can do that for myself whilst shit-faced and alone.'

I suppress a smile. 'Of course you can. I didn't mean to suggest otherwise.' I take a breath. 'It's just...'

'Go on, Dasher, spit it out, I can tell you're dying to bestow on me whatever wisdom you think I need to hear.'

'I just wondered whether you do things because of the way

you think they look to other people, rather than because they make you happy.'

'That's deep.'

'Not really. Just a sixth sense I have about you.'

'Uh huh.'

'Don't forget, I know how much your brother and sister compete at life and how they've dragged you into doing the same thing to try and keep up with them.'

'Wow, really going for the heart of the nuclear family angst there.'

I shrug again. 'Okay. Feel free to ignore whatever I say. I'm just trying to put some outside perspective on it.'

'Sure. Okay.'

He closes his eyes and tips his head back till it touches the head cushion behind him, then opens his eyes again and stares up into the dark night sky.

'You know what *would* help me right now?' he says, still staring upwards into the vast inky blackness pricked with dots of light from the stars.

'No. What?'

'Knowing that you didn't come as hard with your idiot ex as you used to with me.' Tipping his head towards me, he looks me in the eye, then winks.

I let out a snort of laughter, which has bubbled up from the pit of my stomach. 'You're wild.'

He looks at me and grins. 'Yeah. Pretty fucking wild still. Like an animal. I just don't seem to be tameable.'

I let out another giggle. He smiles, then starts laughing too.

'Look at the pair of us. What a couple of limes.'

'Limes?'

'Yeah. Green on the outside and bitter on the inside.'

The absurdity of this statement makes me laugh harder,

and I'm suddenly caught in a kind of emotional hysteria. But I can feel it starting to tip into tears, so I squash it down quickly and pull myself together before it gets a hold on me. The very last thing I want to do right now is start bawling in front of Kit.

'What exactly were you expecting to happen when you invited me to come here tonight?' I blurt, still trying to recover myself.

He holds up both hands. 'I had no expectations. I just wanted to keep talking to you.'

'Uh huh.'

'Seriously. Feel free to leave at any time if you're not having fun.'

'I am.'

'What? Leaving?'

'Having fun.'

'Good.'

We grin at each other, until I feel my face getting hot and have to look away.

'You know, Adrian was always jealous of you. He hated it if anyone even mentioned your name,' I say, staring down into the bubbles in front of me.

'Anyone? Or you?'

'Anyone.'

'Well, the feeling was mutual. The guy was a dickhead – still is by the sounds of it. I could never understand why you'd finish with someone as *incredible* as me' – his eyes twinkle with mirth – 'and then get together with someone like *him*.' He pulls a face. 'From the couple of times I was in his vicinity he seemed like the most boring fucking dude on the planet.'

I wrinkle my nose. 'He's not boring. He's just not as *spontaneous* as you.'

Kit snorts and turns away, shaking his head, then turns back a moment later to fix me with his dark gaze.

My stomach flips at the sight of it. I've seen this look on his face before. And it always led to something exciting happening.

'Okay, how about this for spontaneity,' he says. 'Wild idea. Very fitting. We should have revenge sex. Just for recreational purposes, no strings. We can make sure it gets back to him, if you like? I can tap up some contacts and get the news shoved right under his nose. I'm more than happy to play the part of the hot lover you could never forget and just can't resist boning now.'

I close my eyes and shake my head in jokey disparagement, though beneath the water, my whole body has just responded in a way that makes me wonder whether it's not *such* a bad idea.

But it is. A bad idea, that is.

'Jesus. Your ego didn't get any smaller, did it?' I joke, desperately trying to get my longing under control.

His grin is wide and wicked. 'We did have great sex though, right? Admit it.' He looks at me intently from beneath his long, dark lashes. 'I know you think we're not suited personality wise, but there's definitely sexual chemistry between us. It's still there. I'm not imagining it. Am I.' It's not a question.

I swallow and find my mouth is suddenly dry. 'No. You're not.'

'So? How about it?' he murmurs.

My body is screaming *yes please*, but my common sense is telling me *not a good idea*.

'I'm really not looking for another relationship right now. I'm too bruised,' I say. My voice sounds rough and breathy. It must be such an obvious give-away that I'm struggling with that as a decision.

'I'm not asking for one.'

Uhhhh. He's *not* making this easy.

'I don't know if it's a great idea though, Kit. I came here to get my head together and spend a bit of time on my own.'

'And you can. I promise you, I'll give you as much space as you like. I'm not looking for anything serious either. Just a bit of fun. I swear.'

I can't tear my gaze away from his. It's mesmerising. Because my body has remembered exactly how much it loves to be close to his.

I'm so confused right now. I know I shouldn't be feeling like this. But I am. I just *am*.

'A revenge fuck *could* be cathartic, for both of us, I guess,' I say, my voice still breathy, like I've just sprinted for a mile.

'That's the spirit,' he says, leaving his side of the tub and moving slowly towards me, his gaze intent on mine.

My heart starts to race.

He reaches my side a moment later and I feel the hard plane of his stomach press against my knees.

My skin is on fire with a long-forgotten yearning, and it's so sensitive even the small part of him that's touching me is sending a riot of lust rushing through me.

'We're acting positively,' he murmurs, pushing gently against my knees, so I'm forced to part my legs. 'Reclaiming our equilibrium.'

He moves closer, his torso now pressing into the insides of my thighs, and props his hands on either side of me against the rim of the tub.

He's gazing into my eyes, his intention to kiss me very clear.

I feel happy and sad and turned on all at once and it's a bit too much to handle right now.

'But I'm not convinced it's a good idea for us to do it *together*,' I mutter, staring right back at him.

He cocks his head and blinks at me, as if surprised by my statement, then backs away, pushing away from the side with his hands and out from between my thighs, putting some space back between our bodies.

'Well, no pressure. I'm happy to leave it here and say goodnight if that's what you'd prefer. Your choice.'

His chest is rising and falling and I can tell he's turned on, but trying not to let it intimidate me in any way.

He's a good guy and I know I can trust him to respect whatever decision I think is best for me.

Which is probably to stop taking this so seriously and allow myself that fun I've been craving.

So I take a breath, swallow hard and say, 'I choose that you carry on doing what you were just about to do.'

Pleasure sparks in his eyes and the corner of his mouth lifts into a lopsided grin. 'Good choice, Dasher. Good choice.'

He keeps his gaze locked with mine as he dips his hands into the water and a second later, I feel his fingertips skim the backs of my calves, starting at my ankles and moving slowly up towards my knees.

My skin is alive with sensation again and my pussy throbs with need as his touch works its magic on me.

Tingles. All. Over.

'Is this okay?' he murmurs, still looking deep into my eyes.

I can't break my gaze; it's like I'm locked in place, trapped in his thrall.

A pulse beats hard in my throat and my head swims. It's not just from the wine either, it's lust. Pure and simple. He always could turn me to jelly just by touching me.

'Yes,' I manage to reply, my voice breathy and low.

His hands move higher, then sweep around to the outsides

of my thighs, and he begins to walk his fingertips deliberately slowly up towards my tankini.

'You've got such incredible legs,' he murmurs, 'I can't wait to feel them wrapped around me again.'

My heart leaps and I swallow hard as his fingers find the elastic at the top of the tankini bottoms and he tugs at them, pulling them down my thighs inch by inch, as if he's savouring every second of the action.

His dark eyes are still fixed firmly on mine as he moves back a little so he can slide the swimmers all the way down my legs and over my feet, then scoop them out of the tub and toss them onto the side behind me.

He moves towards me again and I close my eyes, thinking he's going to kiss me. But he doesn't. Instead, I feel his hands grip under my ribcage on each side of my body and he lifts me up and out of the water so I'm now sitting on the edge of the tub.

I lean back and brace my hands against the decked floor behind me to keep me semi-upright so I can see what he's doing.

Running his hands down the sides of my body, he scoops them around to the insides of my thighs and pushes my legs open, so I'm sitting there fully exposed to his gaze.

It's both nerve-wracking and incredibly erotic as he stares at me in what looks like intense fascination.

'Fuck, Dasher,' he grinds out. 'I'd forgotten how beautiful your pussy is. I have to get my mouth on it right now.'

Before I can respond, he leans forwards, moving his head between my thighs.

I feel the heat of his breath on me for a second before his tongue sweeps slowly and lightly along the seam of my pussy from top to bottom, as if he's re-exploring every inch of it.

Reminding himself of my contours.

Pricks of light flash behind my eyes as sweet sensations flutter through me.

His breath is on me again as he draws back a little and then starts another long, slow sweep, stopping for a few seconds at my clit to swirl his tongue around it a couple of times, before flicking over it, making my legs jump on either side of his head with the exquisite pleasure of it.

A long, low moan escapes from the base of my throat.

He takes my vocal appreciation as encouragement and begins to flick his tongue more quickly against me, every now and again taking a second to suck down on my clit, making me arch my back with the intense joy of it.

I'm so aware of how hot and needy I am between my legs. How turned on and slick with lust I am.

I want more. So much more.

I'm almost dizzy with it.

To my relief, I feel him slide his hands up my inner thighs to my pussy and he uses his fingertips to part my folds and open me up to his exploration.

The feeling of being handled so confidently like this is incredible.

Then one of his fingers slides easily inside me and he presses downwards, in the way he knows I love.

It's so familiar a feeling, yet also so alien, my mind starts to spin. I have that sensation again that I've stepped into a parallel universe. Or maybe gone back in time?

Whatever it is, it pulls me out of my total physical absorption and brings me back to the side of the hot tub where I'm aware of my wrists aching a little from the pressure of me leaning on the heels of my hands, and of the cool night air on my exposed skin, and of the fact that I'm out in the open, with Kit going down on me.

Kit.

The sound of voices and laughter in the distance penetrate through the remaining fog of my desire, and a sudden wave of acute awareness about exactly what we're doing washes over me, killing my carefree mood.

This is crazy.

I'm only days out of a relationship – an *engagement*, for fuck's sake – and I've already got a guy's head between my legs. Not just any guy either, a dangerously attractive guy with whom I have no real chance of a future.

But isn't that the point?

Angst is working its way up from my stomach to my throat now though, like creeping acid, and I'm suddenly hit with the clear realisation that I should stop this.

It's not the right time.

'Wait, wait. Actually, this is – it's going too fast. It's too soon,' I blurt.

Kit pauses what he's doing and looks up at me, a concerned frown on his face. 'You sure? Obviously, if you want to stop, we'll stop.'

The sudden loss of his deft touch is torturous and for a second, I consider telling him to ignore me and carry on. That I made a mistake.

But I don't. I'm clearly not in my right mind just now to let this go as far as it has. Though I don't blame Kit one bit. I agreed to it. It's on me.

'I can't.' I can feel my frown creasing my forehead. 'I shouldn't.' I shake my head, trying to wake myself up from the lingering dream state I've been in. 'I should go.'

'Okay,' he says, fully backing away from me now and holding up both hands as if in surrender.

'Yeah. Thanks.'

I reach behind me and snag my tankini bottoms with my fingertips, then proceed to pull them back on, my fingers fumbling and clumsy.

'If you change your mind, you know where I am,' he says.

'I won't.'

I stand up unsteadily, my legs like jelly.

'Okay.'

Turning back, I give him a beseeching look, holding my hands open on either side of me. 'Look, it's just—'

He raises his own hands again in a display of capitulation. 'You don't need to explain. It's fine. Really. No big deal.'

I nod jerkily. 'Okay. Thanks. I – err...' I suck in a breath. 'Bye, Kit.' Then I turn and stumble away from him, not looking back.

'See ya, Dash,' he says behind me.

6

KIT

Well, that didn't end the way I was hoping it would.

I think in my semi-intoxicated state I'd had a mad idea about proving to her she was better off without that loser, Adrian. That there are far better lovers, better men. Like me.

But, whatever. There was no way I was going to push her to carry on. She's clearly having a hard time getting past the emotional havoc that shithead wreaked on her and I don't want to add to that.

I'm pretty sure her agreeing to come back to mine this evening wasn't all about getting one over on her prick-of-an-ex though.

I got a good boost to my self-esteem anyway, from knowing she still finds me attractive. That there's definitely still a connection there.

Even though things hadn't finished badly, five years ago, I'd still been a bit cut up that it hadn't worked out between us. I'd really liked her. Unfortunately, she'd wanted to get more serious and I really wasn't in the market for that kind of commitment at the time. I wanted to live large during my uni years. At least, that's what I'd told myself.

I'd thought about her a lot after we split though and wondered whether I should have tried harder to make it work.

Still, no point in hanging on to regrets, as I pointed out earlier.

Shame I didn't get to make her come tonight though. I'd always loved seeing her lose it after holding herself back so tightly. That had been a big part of the fun when we used to have sex – the teasing and the winding each other up and the battling to get the other to relent and let go.

Anyway, I'm choosing to take this evening as a positive healing experience, just like my therapist would encourage me to. I'm moving on with my life. Forging ahead. Re-discovering the fun.

I've lived with the shitty way I've been feeling since Katya left for long enough. It's time to concentrate on my emotional wellbeing now.

With that in mind, as soon as I wake up the next morning, I go straight out to the pool and do fifty lengths, then scoff down the meal that's been laid out in the dining area of the apartment for me. It's a traditional bento breakfast and it's a thing of beauty, with each small dish presented on its own tiny, delicate plate or bowl. There are colourful pickles to go with the grilled fish, curls of crispy seaweed, pretty pink and white narutomaki fish cakes, steamed rice and a cup of miso soup to wash it all down with, followed by green tea.

I feel positively healthier after eating it all.

After taking a quick shower I call my driver to pick me up and we head into the city.

I'm going to stay busy today. Focused on myself. Occupied.

*** * ***

The Kinkaku-ji temple in all its golden magnificence is a sight to see. The gold leaf it's decorated with is so luminescent it hurts my retinas to look at it. Not that I can bring myself to look away.

And the gardens it's situated in are fucking magnificent.

It's *dazzling* here.

No wonder it's such a popular place to visit.

Walking around it, I'm conscious that my skin feels prickly, in a weird kind of way.

Every time I catch a movement out of the corner of my eye, I get a rush of awareness all the way up my spine.

My brain keeps telling me I'm seeing Chloe in my peripheral vision, but whenever I allow myself to turn and look, it's never her, just some other woman with hair a similar colour to hers or with her height and build.

It's really busy here with European tourists too, so it's happening constantly.

Leaving the temple, I go to buy some noodles from a pop-up food stall in a public park and eat them on one of the communal picnic benches, exchanging a few friendly words with a bunch of other tourists – something I've not done in a long time. It brings it home to me that I spend most of my time now in exclusive, top-flight restaurants or behind roped-off VIP sections with other uber-wealthy people intent on removing themselves from the general public.

I'd forgotten what fun it could be to shoot the shit with a bunch of down-to-earth strangers.

After I finish eating, I go for a wander around the streets of Kyoto for another hour or so.

But nothing really grabs my interest.

I'm feeling oddly on edge, like there's something else I

should be doing – some unfinished business – and it's messing with my head.

Eventually I think *fuck this* and head back to the hotel. Sightseeing was never my bag and it definitely isn't today, not when I'm in this mood.

As I walk back through reception, I'm aware of a hubbub of noise coming from the direction of the bar. I stroll over, curious to see who's in there and what's going on.

It's the group of women who smiled at me in the pool yesterday. They've all got cocktails in front of them and are laughing away at something one of them has said.

'Hey, gorgeous, want to join us for a pre-dinner drink?' one of the women calls, flashing me a brilliant smile. Her accent sounds Transatlantic American and she, like the rest of them, is clearly well monied judging by the way she's dressed and styled.

I pause for a second, wondering whether it's a good idea. But they all seem genuinely friendly and welcoming, and I'm definitely in need of a diversion right now, so I decide *what the hell*.

'Sure. I'd love to,' I say, strolling over to where they're sitting.

The woman with perfectly styled red hair points to a free chair next to her. 'Come sit with me,' she purrs.

Walking round to the chair, I pull it out and sit down, turning to smile at them all in turn. There are seven of them in total.

Lucky seven.

'Are you here on a hen do?' I ask.

They all laugh uproariously at that. 'Divorce party. Well, a week-long celebration of Tana finally getting free of her limpdick of an ex-husband,' the woman with a long shiny sweep of dark hair says, giving me a slow wink.

'Are you from New York, by any chance?' I ask with a grin.

She grins back. 'Sure are. How about you, honey?'

I lean back in my chair and fold my arms. 'London. I'm based in South Kensington right now but I'm selling up and moving out.'

'Oh, yeah? Where to?'

I shrug. 'I don't know yet. I'll probably stay in central London but I'm taking some time out to think about it.'

'Bad break-up?' the woman with a sleek, honey-blonde bob asks me, her expression a mixture of sincere concern and intense curiosity.

'Pretty bad. We were going to get married. It was her choice to end it.'

There's a general murmur of condolence. 'Sorry to hear that, sweetie.'

'But now you're here with your beautiful new girlfriend?' a woman with shocking pink lipstick says from across the table.

I frown at her, confused. 'Sorry?'

'The woman you were with at the pool yesterday. Is she not your partner?'

I huff out a laugh, a strange sense of longing rushing over my skin. 'She used to be. A long time ago. Not any more.'

They all look at me with surprise and curiosity on their faces. 'Shame. You make a gorgeous couple,' the redhead says.

'I always thought so,' I agree.

'Ooh. There's a story in there somewhere. Care to share it with us? We love a bit of gossip!' the blonde says.

Again, I pause. But maybe talking about all this with a bunch of friendly strangers is exactly what I need right now.

It feels good to be the centre of attention anyway.

'Let me get myself a drink and you all another round and I'll tell you all about it,' I promise, rising from the table and heading over to the bar.

* * *

Chloe

This is not how I expected my visit to Japan to go.

I was all set to spend the majority of it alone, processing my feelings about the end of my relationship with Adrian and coming to terms with the fact I'm now single – and free – though not in the place I thought I was going to be, both emotionally and physically, at this point in my life.

But no. Bloody Kit had to turn up and destroy my plans like the wrecking ball he is.

I don't even know how to feel about what happened between us last night. At the time I wanted it to happen, so much, but now I'm wondering whether it was a huge mistake to let myself get so close to him again.

He's always made my head spin. It was one of the reasons I split up with him five years ago.

I felt so out of control and *consumed* by my craving for him. It was disconcerting. Especially because he didn't seem to feel the same way about me.

After giving myself a talking to, I pull it together and head into Kyoto to look around the centre of the city, trying to keep my mind on the things I'm seeing and experiencing, instead of how my body is still humming with a long-ignored need that Kit's woken up in me.

It's a buzzy city, full of tourists, many of them dressed in traditional kimonos with tabi socks and zori sandals, which I discover can all be hired for the day from a number of shops on the main streets.

I consider hiring an outfit myself, but decide against it for now. I'd feel a bit strange walking around in it on my own.

This, of course, makes me think about Kit again.

He'd probably be encouraging me to do it if he was here. He was always up for a laugh.

I think Adrian would have probably told me to go ahead and do it too, but he would have said it to indulge me, rather than actually understanding the fun I saw in it. And he'd have been a bit uncomfortable walking around with me dressed like that. He's always been pretty reserved about how he – and by extension I – appear to other people. I've found this frustrating at points, but I could usually jolly him out of it. It was always an extra effort I could have done without though, if I'm being honest.

At the thought of Adrian, a wave of grief-tinged tiredness hits me from out of nowhere and I decide to call it a day on the sightseeing for now and head back to the hotel.

Perhaps I should take a quick nap, then have a swim before dinner. Pamper myself a little.

I try not to think about what Kit might be up to tonight. No doubt he'll be flirting full-force with some of the rich and polished women I saw at the pool yesterday. He's never been one to let anything get in the way of him having a good time.

I jump on one of the local trains back to the town nearest the hotel, making a note of where the bamboo forest is located on my walk back. I plan on getting up before dawn tomorrow and arriving there just as the sun is rising.

The stroll back to the hotel along the river soothes me, the rushing of the water a balm to my ears after the busy noise of the city, and I experience a swoop of pleasure at being here in Japan. I've heard people, who have holidayed here, rave about it for so long and I can't quite believe I'm finally here myself, and that it's just as wonderful as they said it was.

Despite all that's happened to me recently, I feel an intense gratitude for the life I have. There are so many positive things in it and I'm confident I'll be able to get past Adrian's betrayal eventually and form it into a new shape. A stronger one.

Maybe Sadie's right. I should treat the split as an opportunity to reassess what I want from life, then take it in a new, exciting direction. Whatever that may be.

Right now I have absolutely no idea.

Stepping back into the hotel, the first thing I hear is the sound of low male laughter coming from the direction of the bar, which is on the far side of the vast reception, by floor-to-ceiling windows that look out over the river.

I'd know that laugh anywhere.

A strong sense of bitter-sweet nostalgia washes over me, and a tingle that starts at the base of my spine rushes up my back and travels over my skin, making me shiver with pleasure. But there's another feeling underneath it too. Something a bit like jealousy. Which is crazy. I don't care who Kit is laughing with. It's none of my business and he has every right to have a good time without me.

We're not even really friends, let alone partners in any sense. Not even fuck buddies, after my abrupt halting of proceedings last night.

Still, I'm inexplicably drawn towards the bar, just to see who it is that's made him laugh like that.

As I get closer I see, as I predicted, that he's sitting with a group of women from the pool yesterday and they're all focused intently on him as he regales them with a story or a joke – I'm too far away to hear exactly what he's saying.

I'm fascinated by how much more grown-up he seems now. How confident and self-assured. How in control of his own universe.

It's really hot.

I watch him come to his conclusion, then lean back in a satisfied manner as the whole group around him burst into laughter.

It's at this moment he looks towards where I'm standing, watching him, and our gazes lock.

An image of his dark head moving between my legs flashes through my mind and my breath catches in the back of my throat.

Before I can turn away, he raises his hand in greeting, excuses himself to the women and gets up from the table, making his way very deliberately towards me.

I'm rooted to the spot.

It would be too rude to just walk away now, but I'm suddenly feeling a bit shaky about talking to him again. Especially after what went down between us last night.

Still. Too late now.

He reaches me a moment later, his smile wide and relaxed.

My heart is racing now and I twist my fingers into my skirt to centre myself.

'Hey,' he says. 'You been out?'

'Yeah. I went into Kyoto.'

'See anything of interest?'

'Lots.'

He nods, seeming pleased to hear I've had a good time.

If only he knew the truth.

But I'm not about to let him know how restless, lost and distracted I've been feeling today.

'How about you?' I ask him.

'I went into the city too. And to the Kinkaku-ji temple. It was really beautiful.'

'Yeah?'

'Yeah.'

But there's something in his body language that's giving me pause. Is he pretending he had more fun than he did too?

'Hey, do you fancy joining us for a drink?' he asks, gesturing back towards the bar and the gaggle of women who are trying to look as if they're not watching us, even though they clearly are.

'Nah. I don't want to intrude,' I say, wrinkling my nose.

'You wouldn't be intruding. Come and meet my new friends. They're a lot of fun.'

'You're okay, thanks,' I say, taking a deliberate step backwards. I can smell his distinctive, spicy aftershave and once again the memory of how much pleasure he'd been giving me with his mouth last night comes slamming back into my head.

I'm uncomfortably aware of heat rising from my chest and up my neck.

Any second now he's going to know just how affected I am by his presence.

And I really don't want him to know that.

It's a matter of self-preservation.

So I have to get out of here.

'Have a good evening. I'm off for a nap,' I mutter, not meeting his gaze now. Before he has chance to say anything else, I turn away from him and head quickly across the reception.

'Dasher!' I hear him call behind me, just as I'm about to reach the corridor leading to my room.

Reluctantly, I stop in my tracks and turn to see him jogging towards me.

'Are you okay? You seem a little tense,' he says when he reaches me.

I swallow, aware of how dry my mouth is. 'I am.'

He pinches his brows. 'Okay? Or tense?'

I sigh. 'Both.'

'Why tense?'

There's a beat of silence where we just look at each other.

I decide I may as well deal with this head-on. It's only going to get more awkward otherwise.

'Look, I'm sorry for running off last night, but I just felt a bit' – I wave my hands around my head – 'spun out. It was wrong of me to be doing that with you, so soon after splitting with Adrian.'

He frowns. 'Says who?'

'Hmm?' I look at him, nonplussed.

'Who are you so bothered about offending with your *terrible* behaviour as a single, grown-up woman?'

'I... err... I don't know! No-one. Everyone!' Frustration and confusion bubble through me. This is not the way I wanted this conversation to go.

'So you're worried that all the friends and family who are here watching your every move at this hotel' – he motions around the empty reception to prove his *bloody annoying point* – 'are going to think poorly of you for having a bit of fun after being fucked over and humiliated by your ex who is now, in your words, "happily off fucking someone else".'

'Yeah, okay. No need to rub it in.'

He frowns. 'I'm not. I'm just pointing out that maybe you should take the advice you gave me last night.'

'What do you mean?' I look at him, confused.

'The point you made about it not being necessary to try and impress other people. That no-one here is actually judging you for your actions and decisions.'

'You think I'm trying to impress my invisible friends by not sleeping with you?'

He shrugs and the corner of his mouth curls up into a wry grin. 'If that's what you want to take from it.'

I stare up at the ceiling and blink hard. 'Ugh! You're doing my head in!'

'Not my intention, I promise. I'm just trying to enjoy my holiday here, Dasher. Not start a fight with you.' He begins to back away from me, heading in the direction of the bar. 'Join in, or not. Your call.'

Then he turns and strides away, his gait relaxed and carefree, as if this encounter is no big deal to him.

He's happily going back to the, no doubt, sycophantic attention he's been receiving at the bar. And will have an amazing night with those women.

Fine. Let him.

Back in my room, I pace around for a minute, straightening things on the low table in the middle of the room, then pick up my phone and check it for messages, of which there are none.

No-one's going to bother me while I'm here, of course. Everyone knows I've come for an escape and to get my head together. I'd let them know in no uncertain terms that I needed space and a change of scene from everyone and everything. That I didn't want to talk to anyone until I was back at home.

I didn't want to be reminded about what had happened with Adrian. Which was ridiculous, of course, because I've thought about nothing else since the moment I got here. Except for when I was with Kit of course.

Memories of last night start to intrude again, but I push them out of my head.

I have to stop thinking about him.

Which is going to be mightily difficult if he keeps turning up everywhere I go in the hotel.

I wonder whether he'll be sat next to me at dinner again.

Knowing Kit, he'll probably finagle a dinner invitation from the women he was sitting with in the bar, then invite them all back to his amazing apartment to party.

Nope. Not going to think about that either.

I take a shower, letting the warm water soothe my frazzled nerves, then blow-dry my hair and dress for dinner.

When I make it to the dining room, which is just as full as last night, I see there's only one free table left and it's mine. There's a boomer-age couple on one side of me and a Japanese family of four on the other. But no sign of Kit and the women.

I give my neighbours a polite nod as I sit down and they return my greeting, then immediately turn away from me, leaving me alone.

Which is exactly what I want.

Right?

Yes.

I distract myself by reading the menu from top to bottom and when the server comes to my table, I tell her my meal choice and order a glass of sake to go with it, trying not to relive the memory of how sexy it had made me feel when I was drinking it in Kit's pool last night.

Argh!

What is wrong with me? Why can I not get him out of my head? I mean, I'm grateful I'm not wallowing in grief right now about the situation with Adrian, but even so. It's wrong to be feeling this way.

Isn't it?

Hmm. As much as I hate to admit it, maybe Kit has a point. Perhaps I shouldn't worry so much about what anyone else thinks about my situation. In reality, probably no-one at all is thinking about me and Adrian or about what I'm doing with myself right now.

My food arrives and I tuck in to it, working my way slowly around the plate.

There's something wrong though. Something lacking.

The food doesn't taste as good as it did last night, when I was dining with Kit. Not sure why. Probably the menu choice I made. It's more fish, which perhaps I'm getting a bit overloaded with?

I'm most of the way through it when it hits me that I'm actually a bit bored, eating on my own. So I finish my meal quickly and thank the server when she comes to clear away my plate, turning down her offer to get me the dessert menu.

When I get up, I realise my legs are shaking a bit and my tummy's started to feel a bit fluttery.

That's weird. It's like my body is in fight or flight mode and is producing way too much adrenaline.

Maybe a walk around the hotel will help.

My feet take me straight to the bar. I guess they have an inkling I'll find something there to help me deal with this restless feeling.

It's busy in there and I do a quick scan of the area.

Kit's not there.

Because of course I'm there to see if he still is.

My heart sinks.

I notice with interest that the group of women are still here though and as I start to turn away to head out of the bar again, my shoulders a little more slumped than they were on my way here, the one with the blonde bob calls out to me, halting me in my tracks.

'Hey, sweetie. Are you looking for Kit?'

I bristle at her presumptuousness, but her manner is friendly and open, so I'm hopeful she's not going to be bitchy to me about it.

'Err, yeah. I just thought I'd pop in to see if he was still around. But I guess not, so...' I start to back away, giving her a tight smile.

She holds up a hand, as if to stop me leaving. 'He went back to his apartment to eat. He was sad you didn't come and join us earlier,' she says with heavy meaning in her voice.

'Yeah, babe, he's really into you. He told us all about your time at university together. It sounded like you both had a lot of fun there,' the redhead says, giving me a salacious wink.

I feel my face start to heat.

'I have to say, you'd make a gorgeous couple,' the woman with jet-black hair says, giving me a wide, genuine-looking smile.

This is so weird. It's like a gaggle of beautiful angels has me cornered and is giving me advice about my love life.

'Err, thanks,' I mutter, at a loss about how to deal with this onslaught of observations.

'I'm sure he'd be real happy to see you if you were to swing by his room,' the blonde woman adds.

As a group, they all nod and smile encouragingly at me.

It strikes me as strange that he'd talk to these women about *me*. I would have thought he'd want to tell them about Katya and the breakdown of his relationship for maximum drama and attention. But it seems not. He chose to regale them with stories of our time together at uni instead.

This, of course, brings back my own memories of how hot and fun our sex life had been. It was brief, but explosive and all-consuming in the short time we were together. Almost like a dream. A fantasy. I guess that's one of the reasons I didn't take it very seriously – it didn't seem sustainable at the time. It was all about the physical, rather than the emotional.

Which had disconcerted me.

Now I'm older and wiser, I'm in a much stronger position to handle something like that though.

But what am I supposed to do now? I can't very well just turn up at Kit's apartment. What would he think?

More to the point, what would *I* think?

I mean, it's not the worst idea in the world, but if I go there now I'm sending a very clear message to him that I've changed my mind about anything more happening between us.

Backing away, I mumble something incoherent like, 'Maybe, I'll see, perhaps later, if he's there, maybe,' then turn and get out of there as fast as my shaking legs will allow.

Back in the safety of my room I finally let my thoughts spin back to last night.

About how electrified I'd felt in his presence.

How being handled in that confident way of his was such a turn on.

Ugh. My head is so messed up...

Though, dealing with a messy head is exactly what I'm here for, of course.

Perhaps his idea about the two of us hooking up and banishing our demons – which have taken the form of our exes' rejection of us – isn't *such* a bad idea.

Neither of us are looking for anything serious from a relationship at the moment, not after being burned so badly by our last ones, so it could just be a laugh.

Maybe this is the stars aligning and giving us both a gift by throwing us together at exactly the right time. Resetting the balance.

It could actually help us feel a bit less shitty and humiliated about our fiancés leaving us.

Like we're taking back control of our own narratives.

A sensible part of my brain decides to stage a quick intervention.

Is this actually a helpful coping strategy? Wanting to shag an ex. Or is it sheer lunacy? Self-flagellation maybe? But a fun kind of punishment. A salve. A distraction from the heavy burden of pain and sorrow I've been carrying around in my chest for the last few days.

I'm so confused.

But I need to see Kit again to try and untangle my thoughts.

I head to his apartment.

7

KIT

I've just finished my dinner, which I ate without really tasting it, and am seriously considering heading back to the bar to see what's going on now and who's about, when there's a knock at the door to the apartment.

Hmm. Who's that going to be? I let my butler go for the night and I didn't tell the Americans where in the hotel I was staying, so, apart from an unexpected staff member, that only leaves one person it could be.

I try not to get too excited as I walk to the door to open it. Just in case. I'd rather not have to deal with any more disappointment right now. I'm already feeling agitated after seeing an online ad featuring Katya in her new modelling campaign for the fashion brand she'd been obsessed with for ages. Her ultimate fantasy. Her dream come true.

How do you compete with that?

I know, I know, I should be avoiding looking at the internet while I'm here, especially social media, but I was bored, okay, and needed a distraction.

Taking a breath and fixing a casual smile onto my face, I open the door.

It's not a staff member.

My spirits rise and my pulse picks up.

'Dash?'

'Don't say anything. Okay? Just... please, don't ask me to explain why I'm here right now. Not yet anyway,' she says, a tight frown creasing the soft skin of her brow.

I blink in confusion, then pull myself together and nod, looking at her expectantly. I don't want to get my hopes up only to find she's here for another round of blowing me off. Rather than blowing me.

Shit, don't go there right now, dude.

'Can I come in?' she asks. There's a weird vibration in her voice that I've not heard before.

I nod again and stand back so she can walk in through the door and past me to the sitting room of the apartment.

She doesn't sit down though, just stands there looking at me, her eyes narrowed and her brow still pinched as if she's angry with me about something.

I'm not sure what I'm meant to have done though. All I did was invite her for a drink with my new friends earlier.

Although, I guess I was a bit lecture-y about the issue she's having with getting freaky with me last night.

But I was only trying to put her mind at rest.

And yeah, okay, maybe trying to change it.

Sue me.

She's clearly nervous and is scratching gently at the sides of her legs in a way that makes me think she doesn't realise she's doing it.

Interesting.

I wait for her to speak, hyper aware she asked me not to question her about why she's here.

I'll happily wait, just appreciating the cool beauty of her until she's ready to talk.

She opens her mouth, then snaps it shut again. Then lets out a frustrated-sounding snort, her lips pressed into a grimace. Her fingers continue to tap at her sides.

Breaking eye contact with me, she turns away and wanders further into the room, reaching out to run her fingertips over the back of the modular sofa. Even when she's edgy about being here with me, her movements are as graceful as ever.

Halfway into the room, she abruptly turns on her heel and quickly strides back to where I'm still standing.

Her gaze snaps to mine again, but this time there's a fierce look in her eyes, like she's made a decision and is determined to let me know what it is.

'Look – can I kiss you? I really want to kiss you right now,' she states.

This I was *not* expecting. But it's not exactly an unwelcome surprise. It's intriguing. And exhilarating.

My stomach tightens and I feel myself get hard.

Because I really want her to kiss me right now. I think I want it more than I've ever wanted anything.

I'm fucking *craving* it, in fact.

So I nod one more time, keeping my gaze firmly locked with hers.

She hesitates for one long, tormenting moment, before taking a step closer to me, then another, until we're only inches apart.

The air's vibrating around us.

My skin prickles with need.

This is sweet, slow torture and I'm loving it.

I really want to reach out and touch her, but I'm not going to. I'm going to let her lead this dance. She obviously needs to. To get some control back over her life, I guess.

Finally, she leans in and presses her mouth against mine, the intensely familiar scent of her filling my senses.

My entire body responds to the light contact of her lips on mine and I have to force myself not to step into the kiss and take over. I want to thrust my tongue deep into her mouth and taste the sweetness of her. To slide my hands over her soft curves. To feel the slickness between her legs coat my fingers.

Fucking hell.

My imagination is already twenty steps ahead of what's happening in real time and I really need to slow my racing thoughts down so we're both at the same speed.

Thankfully, she moves closer, pressing her full, soft breasts against my chest and opening her mouth against mine. I feel the tip of her tongue slide against the inside of my bottom lip, and I force myself to be still and let her explore my mouth, reacquainting herself with it.

We always did kiss each other well. With passion and purpose. None of that annoying nibbling and pecking some people seem to go for.

A low, throaty moan comes from deep within her and I almost lose my cool, managing to hang on by a thread as she presses even harder against me and moves her mouth firmly over mine now, pushing her tongue deep into my mouth.

It's invasive and brilliant and such a fucking turn-on.

I'm *loving* this.

But at the same time there's something bugging me.

I take a second to bring myself back into the room.

She's trembling.

It gives me pause.

I don't want her to be anything less than 100 per cent sure that she really wants this. So I lift my hands to circle her upper arms and gently, but firmly, separate us so I can look her in the face.

'I know you don't want to talk,' I say, my voice gravelly with need. 'But I have to make absolutely sure you're really into this and that you definitely want to have sex with me. You're enthusiastically consenting, yes? I don't want to just assume anything here.'

'Yes. This is me *enthusiastically* consenting to fuck you.'

'Good. Glad we cleared that up. One more thing. Tell me what you want.'

She draws in a shuddery breath, but keeps her gaze locked with mine. 'I want you to fuck me. Hard. Like you used to. I've been numb since it all happened and I just want to *feel* something again.'

I look into her face, wanting to take a minute to reassure myself she really means what she's saying. That she's not going to regret it later.

I see only confidence and resolve in her expression.

'Okay. I'll be back in a minute,' I say, stepping away from her.

'Where are you going?' she asks, sounding a bit panicked, as if she's worried I'm going to hightail it out of a window or something.

'Getting condoms. They're in the bathroom,' I say, flashing her a meaningful smile.

'Oh. Yeah. Of course, good thinking.' She shakes her head at herself, widening her eyes, then rolling them as if she can't believe she was being so obtuse.

'Give yourself a break, Dasher, it's hard not to be befuddled by my charisma,' I joke, wanting to keep the mood light.

It works. She laughs and rolls her eyes at me instead.

'Back in a mo,' I promise, flipping her a grin, then heading into the bathroom.

I close the door behind me quietly, needed a moment on my own to get my head straight before we engage in this madness – which it probably is, to be honest.

Crazy, but necessary?

It was inevitable I suppose, from the moment we locked eyes with each other in the hotel's reception yesterday, that this was where we'd end up. Even if we were both pretending it wasn't.

Staring into the mirror, I check in with myself.

Is this really such a good idea? Especially as we split up before because our outlooks on life are so disparate?

But this isn't meant to be a serious thing, I remind myself. And we're both different people now. More mature and experienced. And unlikely to cross each other's paths again after we leave this hotel.

I'm actually in a much stronger place now, mentally, despite Katya abandoning me.

That suddenly all feels so far away. Like it could have happened to someone else. That's the Chloe effect, I guess. She's a real head-turner.

So this could be a liberation. A proper conclusion to something that's always felt like a loose thread dangling in the darkest recess of my mind.

The entirety of my body is saying, *For Christ's sake, just do it.* My pupils are shot with lust and I'm trembling a bit too. In a good way. An adrenalized, motivated way.

I *need* this to happen right now.

And it'll only be sex.

It's the wrong time for both of us to get into anything heavier.

Yeah, I can do this without getting all emo about it, for fuck's sake.

Grabbing a couple of condoms from my wash kit, I shove them into my back pocket, then check my appearance and give myself one last definitive nod before opening the door and heading out of the bathroom.

Walking back into the living area, my heart pounding in my chest, I come to a screeching halt when I see her standing there waiting for me. She's biting her lip and her fingers are twisted into her skirt. She's the embodiment of explicit sexual need.

It's such an intensely erotic visual my breath catches in my throat.

'Jesus,' I say, without thinking.

'What?'

She looks suddenly worried, like she's afraid I've changed my mind about doing this.

'You're so fucking beautiful,' I say to reassure her. 'I think my legs are going to give way.'

'Ha. Funny.'

'I'm not joking.'

'No?'

'No.'

She lets out a nervous giggle, still looking a bit unsure.

'Come here,' I say, keeping my expression serious.

I like to command.

And I love seeing how her pupils blow out and colour appears on her cheeks as she responds positively to it.

She always did like me in control in the bedroom.

It seems she still does.

Well, good fucking job because that's definitely working for me right now.

* * *

Chloe

I swallow down my nerves and walk towards him, aware how jelly-like my legs are.

This feels so wickedly naughty, but so brilliantly thrilling at the same time.

'Take your clothes off,' he says.

Oohhh, my God. I'd forgotten how much it turned me on to have Kit boss me about in the bedroom.

Adrian never felt comfortable doing it, despite trying it a few times at my tentative request. It all got a bit awkward and uncomfortable, so I stopped asking for it.

It needs to feel authentic for it to work for me, and Kit clearly loves getting into the role of alpha male fuck-master.

Which is very, very good news right now.

Taking a shallow, steadying breath, I start removing my clothes, dropping them onto the floor by my feet, item by item, until I'm down to my underwear.

Just as I'm reaching behind me to unhook my bra, he holds up his hand, then beckons for me to walk closer to him.

I do as he asks, stopping just inches away from him.

He places his hands on my shoulders, then turns me around so I'm now facing away from him.

I shiver with awareness at his compelling presence, imagining I can feel waves of heat radiating from his body towards me.

His unique, delicious scent surrounds me and I draw it greedily in through my nose and deep into my lungs.

My skin is rushing all over, like it's having a pre-orgasm all of its own.

I startle as I feel his hands on me again, sliding deliberately down from the tops of my arms and across my shoulder blades to the clasp of my bra. The bra tightens across my chest as he pushes the hook and eye together, then becomes loose as they uncouple.

I'm trembling even harder now at the anticipation of what's to come. Kit's clearly intent on taking his time about this and is going to make me wait for what I'm ultimately hoping for.

Oblivion.

He pushes the straps of my bra off my shoulders and it falls away from my body and onto the floor by my feet.

My breathing has shortened and I'm acutely aware that I'm making gentle panting noises in the back of my throat.

I feel the air move behind me, then Kit's arms encircle me and he cups my breasts with his hands, using his thumbs to flick over my, now very hard, nipples.

His breath feathers along the side of my neck, right where my pulse is beating an excited rhythm, and it's the most delicious thing ever.

Exquisite sensations ripple through me as he plays with my nipples, giving them little pinches, then soothing them with circular gentle strokes. I've always loved having my breasts touched and he's clearly not forgotten this.

There are echoes of pleasure deep inside my pussy.

I want to feel him there too, but I know I'm going to have to be patient. Kit was never one to rush things.

Just as I start to think I might actually come from the attention he's giving to my breasts, he slides his hands away from them and trails his fingers down my stomach to where the band of my knickers meets my body.

I let out an involuntary moan of pleasure as my whole body shudders in anticipation.

He laughs quietly behind me, the vibration of the sound resonating on my neck.

'I'm loving seeing you so wound up for this,' he murmurs against my skin.

My heart gives an extra hard thump as he walks his fingers lower, down over the front of my underwear to where there's a definite dampness now, from how much this slow exploration is turning me on.

He plays his fingertips up and down the line of my pussy, skirting gently over my clit and making me squirm with the need to be touched with more pressure there.

Before I can push myself harder into his caress, he skims his fingers higher again and I have to bite back a moan of frustration.

But he only leaves me hanging for a few seconds, before I feel his fingertips breach the elastic of my knickers as he slips his hand inside them.

This time his touch is firmer. Just how I need it.

And I can't stop myself from moaning out loud this time.

It feels so good. So, so good.

His fingertips glide over me, lubricated by my desire, and he pushes them deeper into me, opening me up so my clit is exposed and his thumb has full access to it.

My legs twitch as he draws lazy circles around and around it, every now and again brushing fully over the hood and making me shudder with delight.

'Oh my God,' I mutter, pressing myself back against his body and discovering how turned on this is making him too. 'Fuck. That feels amazing.'

To my horror, he suddenly withdraws his hand and pulls it all the way out of my underwear.

'Huh?' I practically shout. 'Don't stop now!'

Again, he laughs against my neck. 'Patience, Dasher. No need to get ahead of ourselves here.'

I'm even more horrified when he backs fully away from me, leaving me standing there, panting and needy and alone.

What the hell is his game?

I half want to know and half don't.

I always loved it when he teased me. It made eventually getting what I wanted, and the resulting orgasm, so much sweeter.

And I'm guessing this is his aim here too.

'Take your underwear off then turn around,' he says, his voice steady and controlled.

I do as he says, pushing my knickers down my legs and letting them pool at my feet before stepping out of them. I kick them away and turn to face him.

Reaching into his back pocket, he takes out the condoms he went to find earlier and puts them with deliberate intent onto the bedside table.

Then he makes me watch as he slowly undresses himself, meticulously removing each piece of clothing, folding it, then placing it onto an armchair next to him, his gaze not leaving mine.

I watch in fascinated awe, my stomach fluttery with need, as I watch his well-defined muscles bunch and flex as he moves. He's so fit and strong-looking. Broad and powerful. Undeniably handsome.

Confident with it too. Which is a turn-on in itself.

Finally, he gets to the only remaining barrier: his underwear. Sliding his boxers down his legs, I watch, captivated, as his cock springs free from its confines. I'd forgotten what a beautiful penis he has. Long and with a preference to hang slightly to the left. And it has an impressive girth.

My pussy gives a throb at the thought of him moving inside me.

I'm so wet now, I can feel the moisture coating the tops of my inner thighs.

Now I've given myself the go-ahead to do this, clearly my body's decided to go all in.

He reaches over and swipes one of the condoms from the nightstand.

'Come here and put this on me,' he says, holding it out.

I walk to him and take the condom from his outstretched hand, trying to disguise how much my fingers are trembling. What's happening to me? This whole situation is turning me into a quivering mess.

But I love it.

Tearing the wrapper, I slide out the condom then look him in the eye, waiting for his nod.

He gives it.

So I reach out and grip the base of his cock with my left hand, using my right to carefully unroll the condom along the length of him, feeling a thrill of pleasure at the sound of his intake of breath at my touch. When it's fully unrolled and he's completely covered, I look up into his face.

He stares back at me with such an intense expression of desire my stomach flips. I think his eyes are entirely black right now.

'Go over there, face the wall and put your hands against it,' he tells me, motioning with a jerk of his head to the area of the room he's talking about.

It's a few steps away from us and my legs tremble as I walk over there with as much grace as I can muster.

The intrigue about what he's going to do to me when I get there is making my blood rush with endorphins.

I'm intensely high from it, every inch of my skin on alert for the next time he touches me.

When I reach the wall, I place the flats of my hands against it and wait there, my breath coming fast and hot through my throat.

I hear his slow, firm footsteps behind me and ready myself for whatever's about to come.

My heart gives a jolt as I have a sudden realisation that I've missed this. So much. This heightened thrill of anticipation and the dangerous pull of desire that actually *scared* me a little five years ago.

But not any more.

It makes me wonder what the hell I was thinking, walking away from it the way I did.

I guess I've grown up in that time and know more about what I want now. What I *need*.

Just as Kit seems to.

The air around me throbs with promise.

I suck in a sharp breath as I feel him grip my hips, then pull me towards him so I'm forced to lean further forwards with my arms outstretched.

'Move your feet wider apart,' he says, his voice gruff and low.

I do this too, walking my feet further away from each other, aware that I'm now giving him easier access to do whatever it is he has planned for me.

There's a beat of silence, where I'm profoundly aware of the rush of my blood and the ache of need between my legs.

Suspended in the moment, I give myself over to it, not moving or saying anything to break the spell.

I'm hyper aware of a rush of air behind me and I brace myself for being touched.

Even so, I start when he moves his hand between my legs and cups my pussy for a moment before turning his hand and sliding first one finger, then another inside me, pressing them forwards and down then crooking them till he finds the perfect sweet spot inside me.

I'm *delighted* to find he's not forgotten how to play my body to perfection.

Wrapping one arm around my middle, he presses himself against my back, skin to hot skin.

I actually groan with pleasure as he starts a gentle tugging motion with his fingers inside me, giving my g-spot the dedicated sort of attention I love, incrementally increasing the pressure and opening me up further to his exploration.

'I seem to remember you liking this,' he murmurs, his voice rough with pleasure.

'Yeah, you've got a good memory,' I pant.

He lets out a satisfied *ha*, which vibrates against my ear. 'I have,' he says, 'luckily for you.' But I hear the smile in his voice.

Cocky bastard.

His ego is the last thing on my mind right now though.

All my thoughts are centred around how amazing this feels, and I give in to it completely.

Bit by bit, he picks up the rhythm and I start to buck against him, the delicious edges of an orgasm beginning to grow and pull together deep within me. I'm close. Very close. So close now I can taste the dark pleasure of it in my mouth.

I'm nearly there.

Nearly.

And then he stills his fingers.

The *evil* bastard.

I swear under my breath, utterly frustrated that I was so close to coming and that he's not going to let me.

Not yet anyway.

He knows exactly what he's doing to me, and I'd bet my life he's loving every second of this sweet, sweet torture he's putting me through.

I suck in a breath as he moves both hands to firmly cup my breasts, then slowly circles my nipples with the pads of his thumbs again. They're so sensitive now I'm getting rushes of electrifying sensation straight to my pussy. It's pleasure on top of pleasure and I'm so desperate for the feel of his cock inside me I'm letting out little whimpers of frustration.

As if he's decided I'm wound up enough now, he moves back against me and I feel the rigid length of his cock press along the line of my pussy.

He's so close. So tantalisingly close to where I need him to be.

There's a moment of exquisite anticipation about what's to come next, where I'm aware of how shallow my breathing has become and how fast my heart is racing.

And then he murmurs into my ear, 'Okay. I'm going to fuck you now. Just the way you like it, Dasher.'

Then he moves back a few inches, lines us up and begins to push his cock inside me.

Slowly.

Very slowly.

Excruciatingly slowly.

He's giving every millimetre of my vagina the attention it's craving, and I delight in the delicious stretch as his substantial girth opens me up, bit by bit.

I let out a long, low breath as I feel him seat himself deep inside me, all the way to his hilt.

He echoes my moan of satisfaction, then just as slowly, starts to pull out of me again.

I gasp in rapture as the head of his cock reaches the entrance to my pussy, then pushes firmly back in again, just an inch or two. He repeats this shallow back and forth motion a few times, driving me wild with the sensation of being entered over and over again with just the tip of his cock.

Then just when I think I'm going to go wild with the need to be fucked, he pushes into me hard and fast, taking himself all the way inside and hitting me deep. I rock forward with the motion, having to stabilise my hands against the wall to take the force of the thrust.

Then again, he pulls out slowly, pauses, then repeats his deep thrust.

He's taunting me, in the best way he knows.

And I'm in ecstasy.

Then something seems to break inside him and he starts to pound into me, slamming me hard, taking me completely, so all I can do is take it. Take his thrusts and every good thing he's giving me.

It's fast and intense and utterly enthralling.

I'm being fucked hard and I'm loving every second of it.

This is my release from everything that's been going around and around my head for the last few days. It's freeing and empowering and orgasmic.

And that's when I come.

Hard.

Harder than I have in a very long time.

Waves of ecstasy rush over me and I totally lose control of my voice, letting out a low, animalistic cry that I'm weirdly only semi-aware of. Lights flash behind my eyes and then all I can hear is the rush of my pleasure, like a waterfall inside my head.

I'm acutely aware that I don't care about *anything* in that moment.

Nothing.

At. All.

In my heightened, insular state I'm only vaguely aware that Kit's still pounding into me, then letting out a low, guttural groan of his own as he comes inside me, his body shuddering its release.

And then there's nothing for a while.

Just silence and peace and calm.

After a minute or so – can it only be that? – I start to come around. It's a bit like I'm waking up from a dream, the after-effects of my frenzy still lingering in the hollows of my mind.

Kit draws himself out of me and I push away from the wall and stumble over to his bed. Flopping down onto it, I roll over so I'm lying flat on my back, looking towards where he's still standing, staring back at me.

Widening my eyes, I give him a lopsided, awestruck smile.

He lets out a snort of amusement, then walks round to the other side of the bed and falls onto it next to me, turning to catch my eye.

'Fuck,' he says on a rush of breath.

'Yeah. Fuck,' I agree.

There's a moment's pause before he says, 'So how are you feeling now?'

'Completely fucked,' I answer.

'In a good way, I hope?'

My answering smile is wide. 'In a very good way. I've not come like that in a really long time.'

'Not since I last did that to you, by any chance?'

'Yeah. I think so.'

He grins back, then reaches over and pulls me against his hard body, enfolding me in his arms and kissing me gently, but decisively, on the lips.

'Excellent,' he murmurs against my mouth.

* * *

Kit

Fucking *yes!*

That's what I'm talking about.

8

CHLOE

I'm sleepy. So sleepy.

It's ridiculously comfortable here in Kit's bed, snuggled up against his solid, warm body, with my back now pressed to his front and his arms wrapped around me.

After getting into his bed, he made me come another couple of times and now I'm finding it very hard to summon the energy to leave it.

I might just stay for a little bit longer and doze, then get up and head back to my own room, since this is a sex-only arrangement. I want to be up early anyway, ready to catch the dawn at the bamboo forest.

But it's going to be hard to tear myself away.

It's so comforting to be held like this – so closely and covetously.

I feel really *wanted* right now.

Which is a relief after feeling like I might never be wanted again – at least not in the way Adrian used to want me.

My self-confidence has taken a huge knock from his rejection and I'm not sure I'll ever fully recover from it. How will I be able to trust a partner again? Because everything I thought I knew and believed and would have staked my life on being real and true all turned out to be a resounding lie.

Out of nowhere, a dreadful sense that I'm about to cry surges up from my chest and I tense my body, fighting it back.

No, no, no! I don't want to let this get a hold of me right now. Not when I've just had such a fun time with Kit and I'm feeling good about what happened with him.

I guess I've been forcing down the mixture of grief and creeping humiliation for so long it's starting to push back – and win. It's been lurking there the whole time, poised and waiting to ruin my time here.

But I'm *not* going to let it.

Every muscle in my body is tense from trying to get on top of this battering-of-sadness, and this seems to disturb Kit because he starts to move behind me, pulling me closer against his body. I feel his breath on my neck, then the soft press of his lips on my skin, right over my pulse point, and despite the angst rushing through me it makes me shiver with pleasure.

'You're not actually a vampire who's going to try and suck my blood now are you? Right when I'm at my most vulnerable,' I joke in an attempt to get a handle on my raging emotions. I really don't want to fall apart in front of him. This thing with him is supposed to be a diversion and a bit of levity for us both, not a foray into our deepest darkest fears.

But he's clearly sensed my stress, somehow, because he says, 'Are you okay? Your whole body's gone stiff. I can actually feel you vibrating.'

'Yeah, I'm fine. I just stupidly started thinking about the wedding that wasn't.'

'Hmm,' he murmurs. 'That sucks. Dark thoughts always choose to rock up in the early hours, don't they? When you're emotionally at your weakest. At least, that's been my experience.'

'Yeah. It's like my psyche's trying to punish me for making bad decisions or something.'

'Well, if it's the cancelled wedding thing you're talking about, I don't think you have anything to be punished for. He's the one who left it to the last second to make the bad fucking decisions. It shouldn't be on you to pay for them.'

I give a little hiccoughy laugh, feeling a lone tear escape from my eye. 'Unfortunately, I don't think it works like that.'

I feel Kit move his arm and the next thing I know, he's gently brushing my hair away from my face and smoothing his hand across my scalp in such a tender gesture I almost start crying for real.

But I manage to hold it in. Somehow.

There's a moment's pause before he asks, 'Were you really happy with What's-his-name though?'

'Adrian?' I pause and swallow down the lump in my throat. 'Yeeees,' I say, forcing my voice to remain steady. 'At least, I thought I was.'

'I only ask because I was surprised when you got together with him. He didn't seem like the type of guy you'd go for.' His voice is tinged with disdain, in a way that makes me believe he thinks I settled for less than I deserved.

'No, well, sure. He was really different to you, which is what I needed at that point. I didn't have to compete for his attention and he made me feel really cared for and wanted.'

Kit lets out a breath through his nose. 'I wanted you.'

I huff out a strained laugh. 'I mean not just sexually.'

There's a long pause, before he says, 'We were good together though, right?'

'If you're trying to get me to say that sex with you was better than with Adrian then you can move along. I'm not here to boost your ego.'

I feel him tense behind me. 'Why are you here?'

I pause and swallow hard. 'Good question. I don't know. I told myself it'd be better to avoid being anywhere near you while we were both here but somehow I've not been able to stay away.'

'Yeah, I noticed.' I hear the smile in his voice.

'All right. Please don't go back to being the entitled prick I accused you of being all those years ago,' I joke.

'*Falsely* accused.'

'If you say so.'

I feel him lift his hand from my hair and rub it over his eyes. 'You know, I wonder whether you took some of the things I said back then a bit too seriously?'

I shrug my free shoulder. 'Maybe. I was a lot more gullible and uptight and a lot less street-smart back then, that's for sure.'

'Yeah. You seem more chill now. I mean, we never could have had a serious conversation back then. We weren't on the same page, emotionally.'

'I think we were world-class at misunderstanding each other back then,' I agree.

'In some ways.'

'Not in all, true.'

'We always seemed pretty much on the same page when it came to sex.'

'We did. And we still are, it seems.'

'I guess the conflicting way we felt actually fuelled how explosive our sex was back then.'

'Yeah. It did. We had some pretty wild times, that's for sure.'

'So we should consider this a re-centring experience for both of us,' he says.

I shuffle around in his arms until I'm facing him. 'Do you think we'll be able to handle this and not get any fallout from it? Be able to walk away as friends when we leave here?'

The skin at the sides of his eyes crinkles as he smiles. 'Of course. As long as we keep to our boundaries so we know what to expect at the end.'

'Yeah, you're right. We should definitely do that.'

'Okay. So what are they exactly?' he prompts.

'We should agree not to try and turn this into anything more than it is right now: a holiday fling with a side order of revenge on our exes.' I flash an evil smile.

'You don't want it to be more?'

I frown and shake my head. 'No. I'm going to need time to heal from what happened with Adrian before I embark on another serious relationship.'

He's staring down at my mouth when I say this and gives a slow nod. 'That's probably sensible.'

'Anyway, just because we're sexually compatible, it doesn't mean we're built for a proper relationship with each other. We need different things.'

He doesn't say anything to this, but after a short pause, he nods again. 'I hear you.'

'So it's just sex. While we're both here. Are you up for that?'

After a second's pause he looks up, straight into my eyes, then slides his hand between our bodies, moving it across my belly, then lower to the juncture of my thighs, where his fingertips start to play a steady rhythm, waking up all my nerve endings.

I suck in a breath of pleasure as the familiar surge of lust fans over me.

'I'm definitely up,' he says with a grin. 'So, just to be clear, if I touch you like this, you're telling me you'd be totally happy with that?' he murmurs.

'Happy? Yes,' I say on a long exhalation.

His touch moves deeper and he uses his other hand to gently push my thighs apart to give him better access to my pussy.

Yeah, I have no problem with letting this happen.

None whatsoever.

I'm aware of my eyelids fluttering as I sink into the blissful sensations he's drawing from my body.

But he's not giving it his all; he's holding back, I can tell.

Deliberately, I'm sure.

My suspicions are confirmed when he murmurs, 'If you want to come, you're going to have to tell me what I want to hear,' in a gruff, singsong tone.

'You're such a smug bastard,' I groan.

But he knows I'm only taunting him in the throes of sexual frustration, because he gives a low, amused laugh and says, 'Oh, I know.'

But *still* doesn't start moving his hand in the way he knows I need him to again.

Dammit!

'Okay, okay! Yes, you're the best lay I ever had,' I say, pushing myself into his touch, not caring now how desperate it makes me seem.

'Good. Cos you're mine too,' he murmurs, finally moving those thick, blunt fingers against and into me in the way he knows I love.

I'm so close already it takes only a few seconds of his dedicated touch pulsing against me, in the most perfect rhythm, before I fall into a well of bliss.

He holds me close as I luxuriate in my post-orgasmic haze,

wrapping his arms around my back and fitting my head into the space between his chin and chest.

My eyes are so heavy now. I feel as if I could sleep for a week. All these orgasms have depleted me, used up the last of my energy.

I'm so warm and snug here in Kit's arms and I'm aware of his breathing starting to become shallow, and the rhythmic rising and falling of his chest slowing as he falls asleep again.

It's so soothing, being held like this. So blissfully calming. So quieting...

And suddenly I'm awake again.

There's a familiar tune playing by my head.

It's my phone alarm.

Wriggling out from under Kit's heavy arm, I grab my mobile off the nightstand and squint at the screen. The alarm I set for a pre-dawn wake-up call is going off.

Oops.

I didn't mean to fall properly asleep here, but I guess my body had other ideas.

It appears, from the slow rhythm of his breathing, that Kit is still sleeping soundly, so I decide the best thing to do is try and creep out quietly so as not to disturb him.

But it seems I'm not creepy enough because as I carefully move to the edge of the bed, he stirs. Then as I get up and search around the room for my clothes, pulling them on hurriedly, he wakes up fully and props himself on his elbows, blinking at me in the moonlight coming in through a chink in the blinds.

'Where are you sneaking off to?' he asks, his voice rough with sleep.

A delicious shiver runs over my skin at the sound of it.

I stop what I'm doing and turn to face him.

'I'm going to the bamboo forest before the sun comes up. Apparently it's the place to be at dawn.'

'Really? That sounds cool. Want some company?'

I pause, thinking about this. Do I? I thought I'd feel a bit nervous about hanging out with him this morning after what we got up to last night, but I actually don't. I just feel vaguely buzzed and a bit sleepy, to be honest. But not in any way awkward around him.

He's looking at me expectantly and my heart does a strange turning-over thing.

I decide that I can't very well tell him I don't want him to come with me, not after how downright cool and friendly he's been towards me recently. And it might be more fun to see it with someone else anyway.

'Sure. If you fancy it,' I say, off-handedly.

He sits up and rolls his legs over to the side of the bed, then gives his scalp a good rub, making his hair stand on end.

Turning back to face me, he shoots me a smile. 'I'm always up for an adventure.'

'Then let's go,' I say. 'We've got to leave right now or we'll miss it.'

'Okay, boss,' he says, getting up from the bed.

He's still stark-bollock-naked and I feel like I've been turned to stone as I watch the beautiful, sensual movement of his muscular form as he gives a big full-frontal stretch right in my field of vision. I'm aware I shouldn't stare at him, but I can't stop myself.

Not that he seems to care.

In fact, when he notices I'm gawping, he raises his eyebrow in an *Ah-ha! Caught you!* way, then flips me a smug grin.

'Busted, Dasher,' he says with laughter in his voice.

'Yeah well, what do you expect? I'm a red-blooded woman

and you're *right there* in front of me,' I say, glad that it's too dark for him to see how hot my face is.

He lets out a bark of laughter. 'That's fair,' he agrees, grabbing his clothes from last night from the armchair and quickly pulling them on.

'Okay, let me brush my teeth and I'm good to go,' he says.

'Hmm. Good idea. Do you have a spare toothbrush by any chance?' I ask hopefully.

'Sure do,' he says. 'And before you freak out, the hotel provided it with the room, I didn't get it specially, hoping I might entice you over here and give you cause to use it.'

'Yeah, whatever you say,' I tease, hoping he takes it the right way.

Luckily, he just lets out a low, gruff laugh at that and makes for the bathroom.

I give myself a mental shake and follow him in.

* * *

Kit

It's the weirdest thing, brushing my teeth side by side with Chloe Dasher after five years of thinking I'd never see her again.

Especially after the way we fucked for England last night, then fell asleep together.

It was immense. Exactly what I needed and a massive boost to my self-esteem to make her come multiple times – giving her the kind of distracting pleasure she obviously needs right now.

I love it when women are vocal about enjoying themselves in bed, and she's particularly good at broadcasting her pleasure.

That was one of the slightly frustrating things about Katya – she was really quiet when she came. Not that I hold that against her, everyone has their own way of expressing themselves, but the sound of someone else's pleasure always intensifies things for me and it's often the catalyst that gets me off.

Anyway, I must stop thinking about sex or I'm going to have a constant hard-on today. Especially if I end up spending it with Chloe.

I don't want her thinking I have a sex addiction.

Once we've finished brushing our teeth we head out of the hotel and walk along the riverbank towards where the Arashiyama Bamboo Grove is located.

There's a subtle glow in the sky now as night turns to day, which feels quite energising.

I know some people get 'the fear' if they're awake before the sun rises – especially if they haven't even been to bed yet – but I've always loved this time in the morning. I'm fascinated by how still and quiet it is, how peaceful. It's like I could be the only human on Earth and it's all there, laid out before me – a world of possibilities.

Not that I'd want to be the last one standing in the event of the inevitable zombie apocalypse that's bound to befall us, considering how much we're messing with dangerous chemicals and DNA.

It's actually a terrifying thought, being left completely on my own. One of my greatest fears, if I'm honest.

'Here it is,' Chloe says, breaking into my uneasy thoughts.

I remind myself that I'm still half asleep after not having slept much, on top of the jetlag that's still got its teeth into me, so it's not surprising I'm feeling so wired and weird.

I'm really happy to be here though. Especially as I'm with Chloe.

There's a look of excited anticipation on her face as we start to walk along the deserted path between the tall bamboo canes.

They must be thirty metres high and get denser the further into the forest we go.

It's still pretty dark, despite the gradual lightening of the sky, but just as I'm about to make a joke about wolves and red capes, the sun suddenly makes an appearance, sending shafts of soft light through the canes and lighting the whole place up around us in a golden blaze.

Chloe turns to look at me in awed wonder and the dappled light plays across her face, making her skin glow and her eyes sparkle.

She's mesmerizingly pretty. It's almost impossible to look away from her. I found the same thing back when I knew her before and I'm finding it doubly so now. Especially here in this magical place. It's like my eyes are magnetically drawn to her.

And I want to touch her. Badly.

But I don't. I keep my hands to myself, not wanting to potentially push her away by being too eager and golden retriever-like.

'You know, the Japanese have a specific word to describe the light shining through trees, which I guess we can apply here too,' she says.

'Oh yeah? What's that then?' I ask.

'Komorebi. It's made up of the kanji characters for tree, shine through and sun.'

'Cool.'

'It really is. Such a beautiful language and such an artistic way to present it. They really have a lot of style, the Japanese people.'

I smile at her enthusiasm. 'I seem to remember you watching a lot of anime when we were at university.'

'Yeah. I still do. I love it. It gives me all the feels.'

I love how passionate she is about the things she likes. It

always fascinates me when people have particular hobbies, especially ones I can't quite understand. I've never felt that strongly about any extra-curricular activities. Unless you include sex.

Which I really should stop thinking about.

I guess it's proving to be true for me: that urban myth about men thinking about sex every seven seconds. It certainly seems to be the case whenever I'm in Chloe's company.

As if she's sensed my deviant thoughts, she grins at me, her expression ecstatic.

Blood rushes to my head and I feel a pulse begin to beat hard in my temple.

Oh man. Something weird and not altogether good is happening to me. I feel properly spun out by the intimacy of this situation.

Maybe this was a bad idea, coming here with her. We're not partners and she's made it very clear she's not interested in having any kind of a relationship with me again.

At the time that she said it, I'd compartmentalised it as a thing to acknowledge but not give any real emotional headspace to. But it's left a niggle in the back of my mind that keeps winding itself into my thoughts.

The thing is, I like her. A lot. And I'm really happy to be spending time with her again.

But I know I can't expect anything more than casual, go-fuck-yourself-ex sex from her.

'Perhaps we should head back to the hotel, before the hordes of tourists arrive and spoil our fun,' I suggest, feeling a strong urge to get out of there and back to a place where I can regroup and beat away these left-field feelings I'm having.

'Yeah. Good idea.' She turns around to face the way we came in, then pauses for a moment, gazing up towards the leafy tops of the bamboo canes. 'I'm so glad I got to see this. It's just as spectacular as I'd hoped.'

'Yeah, thanks for having me along. I would have missed it if it wasn't for you.'

Her smile is warm when she glances back at me, and it makes something twinge in my chest.

She looks a lot happier today than when I first saw her in the hotel reception, that's for sure.

I'd like to think I've had something to do with that.

9

CHLOE

It's funny, but I thought I'd want to do this holiday totally on my own when I decided to still come here after being so unceremoniously dumped, but it's turning out to be much more fun having Kit around to do things with.

In fact, as we stroll back to the hotel together in the soft morning light, for the first time since the non-wedding I feel that maybe I *can* get past the humiliating horror of being dumped so publicly by Adrian.

That I'm going to be okay – eventually.

This distraction with Kit is just what I need to get through the next few days. And maybe beyond. It'll be good to have it in my back pocket anyway. Something to remember when I'm feeling low and lonely.

A shudder runs through me at the thought of what my life will be like once I'm back at home.

Adrian and I have been living together for the last two years and he promised he'll have moved all his stuff out by the time I get back to the UK.

I'm not sure how I'm going to afford the rent on my own

though. My job doesn't exactly pay brilliantly well. But I really don't want to have to look for a new one, even if it means an increase in salary. I love what I do.

'You okay?' Kit asks me, seeming to notice my distraction.

'Yeah. I was just thinking about work, actually,' I say.

At least that's half true. It seems a bit rude to be thinking about Adrian when I'm out and about with Kit. Though I'm sure he'd understand. He's been really kind so far, whenever I've alluded to anything about my car crash of a wedding or my dumpster-fire of a relationship.

His attentiveness and willingness to discuss emotionally intense things has actually surprised me. He was never the type to be serious about *anything* when I knew him at university. He'd always make a joke or turn the conversation to something frivolous – or sexual – if we ever got anywhere near emotion. It drove me a bit crazy at the time. I wanted more depth from him, from our relationship, but he just didn't seem capable of it.

'I was just thinking about how I'll need to ask for a pay rise at work if I'm going to keep paying the rent on my flat,' I say.

'Are they likely to give you one?'

I shrug. 'I don't know if they can afford it. But if I don't ask I don't get. I've been working there long enough for them to not want to lose me, so hopefully they'll seriously consider it, at least.'

'What would you do instead, if you weren't working there?'

'I don't really know. I guess I'd look for work at another environmental charity, since that's where my expertise lies, but there aren't exactly a lot of similar positions I could go for that would pay more than I'm already earning.'

'No, I don't suppose environmental work is a money-spinner,' he says, his brow pinching.

'Unfortunately not, no. It's essential work, but not well paid.

But it's not really about the money for me. England's experienced a significant loss of biodiversity over the last few decades and it's still in constant decline, despite all the conservation programmes working so hard to reverse it.'

I wrap my arms around my middle, feeling my usual sense of overwhelm when I talk about what needs to be done.

'Ancient trees need a lot more protection than they're currently being given and we need to step up the number of new trees being planted too, amongst many other things,' I go on when he doesn't say anything. 'Trouble is, the whole enterprise needs a huge injection of money and effort to turn it around, not to mention more serious support for policy changes. We need to act fast, before the 2030 deadline' – I glance at Kit now, who's staring straight ahead as we walk – 'the year that's been agreed for reaching the targets set to stop the decline in species and protect 30 per cent of our land and sea for nature. We've got a massive job on our hands. Massive.'

'It sounds like you're really passionate about what you do,' he says quietly.

'I really am. I'd be devastated to give it up. There's a lovely family-like atmosphere between the staff where I work and it's so great to feel we're all working towards a common goal.'

'Yeah, sure,' Kit murmurs.

I bristle as I wonder whether I'm boring him. It certainly seems like his thoughts are far away.

But maybe he's just tired. We were up late and then I dragged him out of bed before dawn.

The thought of this brings it back to me how exhausted I am, and I let out a loud yawn behind my hand.

'Time for some breakfast and an enormous coffee?' he suggests, looking over at me. 'Or are you going back to bed?'

'Hmm. It's tempting, but I'm on a tight schedule, which I

need to stick to if I'm going to do everything I've planned while I'm here. So I choose breakfast.'

'Right,' is all he says to this.

'What are your plans for the rest of the day?' I ask tentatively as the hotel comes into sight in the distance. I don't want to seem too clingy, but I wouldn't be totally against spending more time with him today.

Now I'm getting used to his company.

'I thought I'd get my PA to book me a private boat ride down the river. Fancy coming with me? You'd be welcome to,' he says, turning to raise questioning eyebrows at me.

I pause. As much as I'd like to keep hanging out, I don't want to miss out on the things I've arranged and I'm looking forward to.

'Thanks, but I already have a boat ride booked,' I say. 'It's at two o'clock. It's not a private one though, obviously.'

'Oh, right. Where does that go from?'

'From Kameoka.' I pause, wondering whether I should say what's on the tip of my tongue. I decide just to go for it. There's no point in pretending anything at this point.

'You know, I have a spare ticket if you'd like to come with me,' I say. 'I booked for Adrian and me to do it together and they wouldn't give me a refund for his ticket because it was outside the timeframe they allow for cancellations.'

'Seriously? You wouldn't mind me tagging along?'

'Nah. It'd be a shame to waste the ticket. Come and be with the real people, billionaire. You might have a lot more fun that way, instead of pretending you'd rather be on your own, which I know is total bullshit.'

He lets out a bark of laughter. 'You know me too well.'

'Yeah, I do.' I flip him a grin.

'That's the thing about being really wealthy,' he says. 'It's kind of hard to spend the money sometimes.'

I roll my eyes in jest. 'Yeah, that sounds really tough. Such a hard life you lead. I'm not sure how you cope, to be honest.'

'No, hear me out before you judge me,' he says with a sting of hurt in his voice. 'Most of my friends, other than Elliot and Raffa, don't have the same sort of liquid wealth that I do. So if I want to go on a five-star holiday I'm limited as to who I can ask to come with me.'

'You could always come down to their level, you know, and do something cheaper.'

'Yeah, I know, and I do. But sometimes I want to have a blowout and treat myself, but I have to do it alone.'

'So you're telling me that being a billionaire is lonely?'

'It can be, yeah.' He holds up a hand. 'I know, I sound like a total dick right now. One per cent problems and all that. But I can't even offer to treat anyone and pay for them because it can be a point of pride thing. People don't want to be paid for, it dings their own sense of status and integrity.'

'Poor little rich Kit.' I jostle him with my elbow.

'Yeah, yeah. Okay. Maybe I deserve that. I know this must sound like utter bullshit to you. But it's one of the reasons I ended up with Katya I think. Because she was more than happy for me to pay for everything and come with me when I wanted to do something that was prohibitively expensive for everyone else.'

'What is it about *prohibitively expensive* that appeals to you?' I ask.

'The sense of winning at something maybe? I'm doing something most other people don't have access to.'

'So it's like being a member of an exclusive club?'

'I guess so.' He winces. 'God, that sounds so crass when I

hear it out loud.' He rubs his hand over his face. 'I guess what I'm trying to say is that I'm starting to recognise that I probably made a bad choice in Katya because she encouraged that kind of thinking. Which for someone like me, who's always felt like he's chasing to keep up with everyone else, especially my siblings, was like feeding a monster.'

'Well, as long as you learned something from it, it wasn't a total bust.'

'Yeah. Maybe.'

We're quiet for a moment.

'So what do you say?' I ask, to break the silence. 'Fancy coming on the boat ride with me?'

He gives me a nonchalant shrug, which I suspect he's putting on. 'Sure, why not.'

'Okay, great. Well, we'll need to get a train over there, so meet me in reception at one thirty?'

'Will do, captain.'

I can't hide my grin at that. 'Great. See you then.'

* * *

Kit

The boat station is busy.

So busy we have to take a ticket and are directed to sit on some hard-backed plastic chairs until our number appears on a TV screen above us. It's a little like waiting for the doctor.

There's a gift shop though – of course there is – so we spend a bit of time looking at the tourist-centric nonsense that we have no intention of buying and at the row of vending machines selling ice creams and drinks.

These seem to be everywhere you go in Japan – pretty much on every street corner.

They have a vending machine for *everything* here.

I'm told you can even buy a single glass of wine from some of them, which pretty much blows my mind.

To be fair to it, the boat ride business is a slick operation and our number appears pretty quickly. We're taken down to where the long wooden boat is moored against the wharf with about twenty other people and given slim lifejackets to put on. Then we're directed to climb into the boat and take a seat on one of the long wooden benches that run from port to starboard across it.

The sun is beating down on us now and I'm glad I thought to put some sunscreen on, though I can still feel the intensity of the rays warming my skin.

A trickle of sweat makes a path down the middle of my back.

We're at the rear of the group of people coming on this trip and Chloe climbs in first, then I follow her and sit down on the bench at the starboard side of the boat. Somehow we've ended up at the prow, sitting directly in front of one of the guys who's going to be taking us down the river using a long pole, a bit like they do in the punts they have in Cambridge.

Only, as we set off, it becomes clear that these guys use the pole at the front of the boat, pushing it down into the river bed then running forwards, whilst pushing back against it to move the boat forwards in the water.

I feel exhausted just watching him.

And not only that, he manages to keep up an amusing running commentary with the guy at the back of the boat who's on the rudder, making sure we don't drift into the bank on either side of us.

It's like listening to a two-man comedy skit.

They're charming and funny and informative about the history and geography of the area in equal measure and it just blows my mind that they do this for a living.

It's a very different life from mine, spending hours inside an office, staring at a computer screen or on the phone.

Chloe seems to be really enjoying herself and is alternately gazing around at the knock-out beautiful scenery, which includes rows of cherry trees in full bloom, hanging out amongst the lush greenery, and watching the fit young Japanese guy who's expertly moving a boat full of people along the river, hitting each of the push points in the rocks at the side of us with his pole in order for us to avoid crashing into them.

I'm hyper aware that I wouldn't have had this experience in the private motorboat that I was thinking of hiring. I'd have been on my own, only glancing at the trees and thinking about what I was going to do when I got back to the hotel. And if Katya had been with me, she'd have been on her phone the whole time, checking out her social media feeds. She's obsessed with them. Especially if she thinks she's going to get a photo or name check on any of them.

This is a million times better. A billion.

Particularly because I'm really appreciating seeing Chloe enjoying herself.

It brings it home to me that I never really felt that when I was with Katya. I guess because both of us always went with the most expensive option, which in retrospect felt cool but wasn't always the most fun. She'd spend most of the time being hyper aware of other people watching us as we lorded it up and was quite clearly performing for them. And because she was used to the finer things in life, it meant there was a lot to compete with in order to have a top-notch, unique experience.

Just as I'm thinking this, the boat dips down into a rapid in the water and a big wave of water sloshes up over the side of the boat and straight into my lap.

I give a yelp of surprise, mostly because the water's bloody cold, but also because it now looks as though I've had an embarrassing accident.

'They did just tell us to hold up the tarpaulin if we were worried about getting wet,' Chloe points out with a barely concealed grin at my expense.

I give her a twisted smile back, telling myself I'll get my own back on her later. Perhaps when we're in bed together again.

At the thought of this, my body gives a deep shudder of anticipated pleasure, and she looks over at me again with a more concerned expression this time.

'Are you okay? Cold?' she asks.

'My crotch is. Fancy warming it up for me?' I joke, laughing when she rolls her eyes at me.

But the idea of having her straddling me and wrapping those long shapely legs around my back sticks around in my head for longer than is decent as we glide through the rest of the rapids without further incident.

I'm distracted from my thoughts when I feel her elbow urgently nudge my ribs and she leans in to say, 'Hey, look. There are monkeys over there on the bank,' with such wonder and joy in her voice it makes my heart flip.

I turn to look in the direction she's pointing and see she's right, there are three monkeys sitting on one of the flat rocks part-buried in the bank to the right of us, casually hanging out and watching as we sail past them.

Well, that's fucking cool.

I turn back to her and smile, acutely aware of how special this shared moment is. I love the unguarded happiness she seems so willing to show me now. There's no posturing here. It's her pure, genuine reaction to something that gives her joy.

And it's cost me nothing.

* * *

Chloe

I'm really glad Kit decided to come with me on this trip.

Especially as I just got to see a huge wave of water land solidly in his lap and his resulting comical reaction.

It was the funniest thing I've seen in a while.

He was a good sport about it though. I liked that. If it had been Adrian that had happened to, he'd have been bitching and moaning about it for the rest of the trip.

So that's interesting.

In fact, having some space from Adrian has actually given me a chance to examine the real shape our relationship was in and stop skirting past the issues I'd told myself to ignore because 'no-one's perfect'.

I'd thought he *was* pretty perfect for me once, because he seemed, on paper, to have everything I looked for in a partner: dependability, a strong work ethic, emotional intelligence and kindness.

But I'm now beginning to realise a lot of that was a smokescreen, not just for me, but for his God-fearing parents too.

Since he was young, he's felt the need to give everyone everything they wanted from him, like a true people-pleaser, but the pressure of this obviously got too much and his real needs and wants finally took over.

When I think about it now, I'm aware I was putting down his

increasing withdrawal, and the distance that was growing between us, to him being stressed about the wedding.

I just saw what I wanted to see.

More fool me.

I wish he'd been brave enough to talk to me about how he was really feeling: trapped into something he didn't really want, or more to the point, in the wrong place at the wrong time with the wrong person.

I'm suddenly aware I've been staring out at the bank with a frown on my face when Kit puts his hand onto my leg to get my attention.

'You okay? I feel like I lost you there for a second.'

I give myself an internal shake and flash him a smile, the skin on my leg where he touched me blooming with delicious heat. 'Yup, still very much here. Just thinking.'

'About?' he asks.

I shake my head. 'Nothing of any consequence. I'm loving this though,' I say, waving my hand at the lush scenery sliding past us as the boat moves into a wider part of the river.

We appear to be making a beeline towards another craft with a canopy stretched above it, which seems to be waiting for us to catch up with it.

As we draw alongside, I see it's loaded with snacks and drinks for the occupants of our boat to buy and consume as we finish our journey along the river. A floating 7-Eleven, if you will.

'Want anything?' Kit asks me as a server on the boat comes within speaking distance of where we're sitting.

'I'll have a peach juice please,' I say, suddenly aware of how thirsty I am after spending an hour on the river in the sunshine.

Kit orders my drink and a Coke for himself and hands mine over, our fingers bumping as I take it from him.

Electric sensation prickles along my hand and up my arm. My body seems intent on responding to his at every opportunity. I've never had this kind of reaction to anyone else in my life, not even Adrian, I realise. It's almost as if Kit and I are connected by some kind of magnetic charge.

What a weird thought.

I'm pulled out of my musings when the shop-boat glides away from us and we continue on our way, our hosts picking up their patter of chatter as we make our final part of the journey back to Arashiyama.

Kit points out our hotel, sitting proudly on the top of the bank, looking beautiful and regal but absolutely part of the landscape as we sail past it. I feel a rush of pride to be staying there.

This is one holiday I'll never forget.

A few minutes later, we come out into the wide mouth of the river at Arashiyama, where the boat docks against a jetty and we all clamber out and stretch our limbs after being so sedentary for the last hour and a half.

'Well, that was awesome. Thanks for bringing me along,' Kit says, drawing me against his body and wrapping his arms around my back in a bear-like hug.

I breathe him in, my senses spinning with a weird sort of confusion that comes out of nowhere. His smell is so familiar, yet so exotic and I can't quite get a handle on how it's making me feel.

I think it's a weird mixture of nostalgia and anticipation.

'You're welcome,' I mutter against his chest, squeezing my eyes shut and for just one moment allowing myself to enjoy being enveloped by him and everything I'm experiencing right now.

I breathe it in, then breathe it out.

Then I disentangle myself from his arms and take a step back away from him.

My stomach feels like it's full of insects.

'Hey. Want to grab some lunch?' he asks, not seeming to notice my agitation.

I pause, still struggling to get on top of all the emotions I'm feeling right now. 'Err, actually I thought I'd go back to the hotel for a bit and rest,' I say, not able to look at him and instead pretending to gaze out across the water to where more boats are appearing and heading towards the dock.

'Oh. Okay. Sure. No problem,' he says, but I could swear there's squashed disappointment in his tone.

I stretch my arms above my head, pushing away the feeling of guilt. I really need a bit of time on my own to recover and regroup. 'My back's still a bit sore from sitting for so long on the plane and just now on the boat,' I tell him, to assure him my disappearing act isn't because I don't want to hang out with him. 'I was hoping to get a massage this afternoon but reception tells me all the treatments are fully booked so I thought I'd do some yoga instead to try and loosen myself up.'

He frowns. 'Fully booked?'

'Yeah.'

I watch as he slides his phone out of his back pocket, and before I can say anything else he makes a call to the hotel and tells them he wants a massage appointment made available for me in an hour's time.

'Oh my God, you didn't need to do that,' I say, half scandalised, half impressed when he cuts the call.

'If I can't use my influence for getting your back fixed what's it good for?' he says with a wry grin.

'I hope I haven't taken someone else's slot,' I ask fretfully.

'You haven't. I have my own personal therapist assigned to my apartment, who's available whenever I want them.'

I swallow. 'Wow. That's cool.'

'It is,' he says with a grin. 'And they're all yours this week. Feel free to use them whenever you want.'

'That's really kind of you,' I say, blown away by his generosity.

I don't want him to think I'm just using him for his perks though, so I say, 'You know, I've been thinking about trying out one of the sashimi restaurants in Pontocho Alley this evening. Fancy coming with me?'

He gives one of his shrugs. 'Sure. I've never had sashimi. That's raw fish, right?' he says, sounding a little unsure about my choice of meal.

I grin at him. 'So I hear. I just wanted to try it once so I can say I've eaten it.'

'Okay. You're on,' he says, this time with more enthusiasm.

'Great, then it's a date.'

10

KIT

Pontocho Alley looks exactly the way I envision old-school Japan used to, with traditional machiya dark wood townhouses crammed together down a narrow street, which bustles with tourists, their path lit by the soft glow of paper lanterns.

If it wasn't for the modern dress of the crowds around us, all super-focused on finding somewhere to serve them their dinner, you could easily imagine you've time-travelled back a hundred years. In my mind's eye, I can even see the ghosts of geishas gliding out of the doorways, it's *that* visceral a scene.

The street is cobbled and uneven so as we make our way down it, we have to watch our step as we dodge between groups of people who regularly stop dead in their tracks to check out menus outside the many eateries.

When we finally decide on which sashimi restaurant we want to try – they all look so inviting it's difficult to know which one to choose – we have to wait until they have room to accommodate us. It's not long until a table comes free though and we're taken to be seated by a large window that looks out over the Kamo river. The nightlights along the riverbank illuminate the slow-flowing water, making it glint in the darkness.

'Well, this is pretty special,' Chloe says, looking around her with an expression of happy satisfaction.

'Yeah. It's great,' I agree, staring down at the menu, which has a huge range of colourful-looking sashimi dishes on it. Even though each one looks like a work of art, in all honesty, none of it looks particularly appetising, but I remind myself I'm here for the challenge of trying something new and different and shouldn't judge it till I've tried it.

So when the server comes to the table to take our order I just stab at a couple of things on the menu, not really having much of a clue what I'm ordering.

Chloe seems to be taking a more thoughtful approach though, because she asks the server about a couple of the dishes before making her choices.

When we're finally left alone, she leans in conspiratorially and surprises me by saying, 'I have no idea what's going to arrive. Fingers crossed it's edible.'

I let out a laugh at that, feeling a sense of relief that I'm not on my own here, having to pretend I'm totally cool about what I'm about to encounter.

We're in this together.

I never felt like that when I was with Katya. She always wanted us both to appear to be super confident at all times.

Warmth floods my chest and I take a long drink of the glass of tap water that was delivered to our table while we perused the menus.

'Thanks for coming with me. I'd feel a bit strange about coming to a restaurant here on my own,' Chloe says, the corner of her mouth twisting into a grimace.

'My pleasure,' I say, meaning it. 'I'm very much enjoying

playing the role of hot ex-lover who's not only great in bed but an excellent dinner companion too.' I flip her a grin.

She smiles back, but I can tell I've hit a troubled nerve.

'Sorry,' I say, 'We don't have to talk about that right now if you'd rather not.'

'No, it's okay. I didn't mean to bring the mood down. It just keeps hitting me at odd moments that my whole life is going to be very different from now on. Not that that's necessarily a bad thing. Just something I'm going to have to get used to.'

Picking up her own glass of water, she takes a sip. 'I suspect there are going to be a lot of people wondering aloud why he did that to me, especially as he comes across as such a good guy.'

I nod in understanding.

'I'm not looking forward to answering all the kindly meant but incredibly awkward questions about how I'm doing when I get back,' she continues. 'I wish I could just stay here where it's simple.'

Yeah, me too, I find myself thinking.

Our food arrives then and we glance at each other and smile before picking up our chopsticks and selecting our first piece of raw fish to try. I watch her face as she chews, aware that the food I'm eating is actually a lot better tasting than I was expecting. In fact it's actually pretty delicious. It seems Chloe's having the same experience because she gives me a surprised smile and picks up another bit of food right away, dips it in the little saucer of soy sauce and eats it.

'Pretty good, huh?' I say.

'Yeah. It's actually really nice. Softer than I imagined it would be and less fishy, bizarrely.'

We eat in silence for another minute or so, but I seem to be incapable of sitting there quietly for long with all the questions

I want to ask her buzzing through my head now that she's started to open up to me.

'Did you have any inkling at all that things with Thingy-ma-jig were going to go tits up?' I blurt, unable to keep it in any longer.

She sighs and leans back in her chair, running her hand through her hair in agitation. 'In retrospect, yeah, I guess I did. But I just kept ignoring my instincts because I didn't want to think about how I was going to explain to everyone that the wedding was off. I thought it would work itself out, I guess. And it became a matter of personal pride that it went ahead.'

'So it was more about not being humiliated than actually wanting to be married to him?'

Her shoulder lifts in an awkward shrug. 'Maybe. I don't know. We were together for four years so I guess I just thought getting married to him was a done deal. We've always been good friends and agreed on pretty much everything, so he seemed like a good choice of partner.'

'Even though he didn't really ding your bell sexually?'

She frowns at that. 'It wasn't that he didn't ding it. Things were fine in bed. Not the most exciting sex I've ever had, sure, but not terrible. I just decided to prioritise being with a good, steady, reliable partner. He seemed like a better long-term bet than someone who made all my sexual fantasies come true but probably wouldn't stick around in the tough times.'

'Except he did neither in the end.'

She rubs her hand over her eyes, then grimaces. 'You don't need to remind me. I'm very aware of how naïve I was to trust him so absolutely.'

'Sorry. I didn't mean to make you feel worse. I guess I'm pissed off on your behalf about the way he treated you.'

I look up from my plate to see there are tears in her eyes, which she's determinedly blinking back.

'You okay?' I ask, worried by the depth of emotion on her face.

She just nods, then puts down her chopsticks and says in a quiet voice, 'I really thought he adored me. He always acted like he did. But I wonder now if that's actually all it was: an act.' Her brow pinches into a tight frown. 'But I don't think so. I think he did really love me, just not enough and not in the right way. And yeah, maybe we would have got bored with each other anyway. I suppose being good friends is all well and good, but maybe you need fire and chemistry too to keep things fresh and interesting as time passes. That's what I've been telling myself anyway.'

'Did you know he was into guys?' I ask, hoping I'm not crossing a line with that question. It seems like she needs to talk though, so I figure I may as well ask it all now.

She pauses for a moment, as if seriously considering this, before saying, 'He told me a couple of years into our relation-ship he'd wondered whether he might be bisexual. Just mentioned it offhandedly one day, then quickly changed the subject, like he was just musing on it, but it didn't really mean anything. He'd had a pretty strict, religious upbringing and I think his parents put the fear of God into him about how they thought being gay was a sin and basically implied they'd cut him out of the family if he ever ventured anywhere near it. So he'd never explored that part of himself.'

'So it wasn't a total shock when you found out about his male colleague?'

'Not a total shock about that, no. And in a weird way I'm happy for him that he finally felt brave enough to engage with what he obviously really wants and needs. It was the lying and cheating part that hit me right in the guts.'

'Yeah, I bet. It was a fucked-up thing to do to you. Especially waiting for your wedding day to come clean about it.'

She nods. 'It was so weird because I was totally calm right after he told me. It was as if someone else had taken over my mind and my body and I was being manipulated like a puppet. I felt almost... excited. Like I was suddenly taking part in an immersive play. I think it must have been the adrenaline that flooded through me. A fight or flight response gone haywire. Then it was like I was outside my own body, watching the whole drama unfold. I went into practical mode and very calmly asked him to tell me all the details. I needed to know every single thing that had happened. How. When. Who knew. It was a coping mechanism I suppose.'

'Yeah, well, we all respond to stressful situations in different ways,' I say with sympathy.

The smile she gives me is filled with pain. 'I'm ashamed to admit it now, but my overriding response was to want to have sex with him. I guess to try and reclaim him or something. Or prove to myself I still had some sort of hold on him. Some control. I feel so humiliated, thinking about it now. He rejected me, obviously, when I tried to kiss him, idiot that I was.'

'Fuck, that's fierce. No wonder you're so cut up about it.'

She lets out a long breath through her nose, her shoulders slumping a little. 'Walking into the room where the wedding was meant to take place and having to stand there in front of everyone in my obscenely expensive wedding dress and explain it wasn't going to happen that day, or any day in the future, was the worst, most humbling moment of my life. But I did it. My voice was shaky, but somehow I was able to get the words out without crying. I was practicality personified.' She flashes me a sad, wry smile.

'I'm actually proud of myself for doing that. I didn't break down and beg someone else to do it for me. It was important to me though, to handle it myself. I had to face it head on. Look it in the eye. Take ownership of the whole shitshow in order to be able to carry on. I would have hated to look back and been even more ashamed about falling apart.'

'Which would have been a reasonable response, considering the trauma of the situation,' I point out gently.

'Yeah, I suppose so. I didn't actually feel the full emotional horror of it all until a day later. But even then, I couldn't cry. I was just… numb. Then the next day, when I woke up, I felt a bit like I was going mad. I just couldn't believe it had happened. That something I was so sure of, so *convinced* I knew to be true, turned out to be a sham. It made me question every other thing – every other relationship I have. When you feel like you can't trust your own instincts any more it's a total head-fuck.'

'I hear you.'

'At least he had the balls to stop the wedding before it was a done deal,' she says quietly now. 'It would have been hellish to have to go through the ordeal of a divorce instead – especially if we'd ended up having kids together.'

Her voice breaks on the last couple of words and tears spill out of her eyes and run down her face. She swipes them away, clearly embarrassed.

My heart goes out to her, and I reach over and cover her hand with one of mine.

'Fuck. Sorry, I shouldn't be talking about this right now. I really don't want to sit here crying in the middle of a restaurant, ruining your night.'

'No need to apologise, Dasher, Jesus. For what it's worth, I think you're really impressive – coming here to Japan on your own. Just getting on with it and moving on. That shows real guts.'

'You're here on your own too,' she points out, her voice broken with tears.

I shrug. 'Sure. But I've had more time to work through my feelings about the end of my relationship than you have.'

This seems to make her more upset though, rather than less, which is what I was actually going for with that compliment. Her face is screwed up now, like she's fighting hard not to sob out loud.

'Hey, do you want to get out of here?' I ask.

She nods, seemingly unable to speak now.

'Okay, I'll get the bill,' I say, then turn away to grab the attention of our server and make the international sign for paying. Then I call my driver to come and pick us up.

Thankfully, we're handed our bill quickly, and I pay up and we leave the restaurant, Chloe forging the way with her head dipped and her loose hair hiding most of her face.

I really feel for her.

Not only is she feeling shitty about the way she was dumped, she's also humiliated about showing it.

I have a strong urge to pull her against me and tell her everything's going to be okay – and then actually make it okay – but I know that's not something under my control, no matter how much money I throw at it.

So I just follow her out and grab her hand, which I'm glad to find she doesn't shrug off, then walk with her back to the end of the road where our car is waiting for us.

She's quiet all the way back to the hotel and I don't say anything either, aware that I might make her cry again with any question I ask.

When we pull up and get out in front of the main entrance, I hang back a little, waiting to see what she wants to do.

Turning, she fixes me with a surprisingly steady smile and

says, 'I'd totally understand if you want to go and hang out with people who aren't killing your mood right now.'

'Do you want me to?' I ask. 'Because, honestly, I'd rather keep hanging with you.'

Her smile widens and her gaze flicks away from mine for a second, then back again. 'I'd like you to come to my room with me,' she says. There's a flash of something in her eyes, like a fire's been lit in her brain.

Is she thinking about our revenge sex pact again?

I hope so.

'Sure. Sounds good,' I say, mentally crossing my fingers, but telling myself not to assume anything.

I actually don't care if we don't have sex.

I just want to be with her right now.

11

CHLOE

I'm hyper aware of Kit walking beside me as we make our way to my hotel room.

I don't think it's fair to just slope off – not that I actually want to do that – but also, it feels like a friendly gesture to invite him to my place this time, instead of expecting to go to his again.

He's not been in my domain yet and I guess I want to let him in a little more. I think he probably deserves that. And I desperately need a distraction from the memories of that horrible day I'd described to him in the restaurant.

I can't believe I cried in public like that.

Letting us into the room, I toss my bag onto the table near the door, then slide off my shoes and line them up carefully, aware of Kit doing the same thing beside me.

Then I walk over and sit on the edge of my bed, feeling it dip as he sits down next to me.

When I turn to look at him, he's gazing at me with his brow furrowed, like he's not sure if he should speak. Maybe he's worried I'll cry on him again.

Or maybe he's not worried about that. Maybe he's genuinely

being a friend right now and keeping quiet so this can play out the way I need it to.

I really appreciated his kindness back there in the restaurant. I really thought he'd hate having to deal with my onslaught of emotion – he certainly would have back in the day – but he was a real sweetheart about it.

It *must* have been uncomfortable for him, but he didn't make me feel stupid or embarrassed about it.

He just took care of me.

It had surprised me. In a good way.

And now I feel like I owe him an apology for ruining his night.

'I'm so sorry about losing it back there,' I say, painfully aware of the shake in my voice. 'I guess talking about it opened a floodgate I'd been holding back. Dislodged an emotional blockage.'

'Emotional blockage. Yeah. I get it,' he says, giving a nod.

'Pretty sexy, huh?' I say, shamefaced.

He grins at that. 'You are, yes, Dasher. The sexiest. And really fucking brave to stand up and face everyone. Especially when the selfish prick shit the bed the way he did.'

I can't help but smile at that and I let out a long, low sigh, feeling some more of the stress I've been carrying leave my body. 'I don't know. He's not really a bad person. He just didn't handle things well.'

'You don't need to make excuses for him, you know. He's a grown man and he should know better than to treat you like that.'

'I don't think he meant to hurt me,' I say lamely.

Kit folds his arms. 'But he did and you have every right to be pissed off with him.'

'I know, but we were friends for so long and, despite everything, I still care about him.'

He frowns. 'But there's no way you'd ever take him back, right?'

I pause for a moment, but I'm sure of my answer to that. 'No. He seems very sure he wants to be with Deacon – the guy he cheated on me with. Anyway, even if he did come crawling back, how could I ever trust him again? I'd always be wondering whether he'd suddenly announce he'd fallen for someone else again. It wouldn't have been so bad if he'd been upfront about how he felt about Deacon when he first started having feelings for him, but he didn't say a word. It's the deceit that hurts so much. I genuinely thought he was my best friend, as well as my lover, and that he'd never do anything to hurt me. But he wasn't and he did.'

'Then think of it as dodging a bullet.'

Trying to order my thoughts, I gaze at Kit, taking in his furrowed brow and the fierce emotion in his dark eyes.

This is a side to him I've never seen before – an emotionally mature side. He's really listening to me and being supportive.

Maybe he's not as self-centred as I thought he was.

He's clearly way more sensitive than most people at uni – including me, I'm ashamed to say – gave him credit for.

But he's hung on to the roguish charm I remember too.

It makes for a heady mix.

This thought brings back memories of laughing with him a lot when we first got together. He had this way of looking at me that just cracked me up every time. A kind of wicked twinkle in his eye. I loved that. It was the most genuine thing about him, that grin, especially when he couldn't maintain his usual *I'm too cool to find anything funny* bullshit act and accidentally showed me his real feelings.

He made me feel like I was the only one who truly understood him when he let his guard down like that.

Not that it happened that often.

We're still gazing at each other and I could swear something changes in his expression. I'm not sure what it is though. It's a subtle shift.

As if he's sensed my confusion, he looks away and leans back on his hands, adopting a more casual pose.

Perhaps this is all getting a bit too emo and downbeat.

I have a sudden urge to wipe my mind clean and start the evening again.

But before I can open my mouth to change the subject, he asks, 'What is it that made you want to settle down so young, do you think?'

I shrug and try to relax my posture too. 'I guess I've always needed to feel absolutely secure about my relationships. My parents set a brilliant example of what a solid, respectful partnership should look like and I wanted that for myself. They met each other at school and they've been together ever since.'

I shift a little, getting more comfortable. 'I always imagined that would happen to me. I felt like it could. It was my ideal. I consider myself a loyal person and when I decide I like you, that's it, you're in.'

'Except when you decide that person *isn't* in any more.'

I look round to catch his eye. 'Are we talking about you again by any chance?' I ask, making my tone light and flirtatious.

His eyebrows raise and pinch together and I see a flash of amusement in his eyes. 'We might be.'

Breaking my gaze, I flop back onto the bed and stare up at the ceiling. 'Yeah well, honestly, when we got together, I really wanted it to work out with you. I really liked you, but it didn't seem like you had the same attitude to relationships that I did and that worried me.'

'Don't you think it's a good thing to have lots of experiences before you settle down though?'

'I didn't at the time, clearly. And I've always been pretty single-minded.'

'No shit.'

I turn to smile at him as he flops down next to me.

'And I'm guessing What's-his-face made you feel like he was as grown-up as you and he took your relationship *very seriously*,' he says, with a hint of droll derision in his voice.

'Yeah, I'd say that was true. He totally love-bombed me when we first got together. I felt really special and *seen*. Wanted.' I smile sadly.

'What a creep,' he jokes.

I have to laugh at that. 'It's all a gamble anyway, right? We can't ever know how things are going to work out.' I prop my head on my hand, my elbow digging into the mattress. 'Can you please use your vast wealth to get someone to invent a crystal ball that actually works so we can see the future? That would be a real gift to humanity.'

'Would it though? Wouldn't life be deathly dull if we knew how everything was going to turn out? We'd just end up spending all our time waiting to die.'

'At least we could prepare ourselves,' I point out.

'But to what end? Especially if you know your time will be up quickly. Imagine living your life knowing that. It'd be torture.'

I think about this for a second. 'But maybe you'd make the most of every moment you had left.'

'Shouldn't we be doing that anyway?'

'Yeah, maybe.'

'Perhaps we'd both lost our sense of adventure if we were

prepared to settle down with our ex-partners,' he says thoughtfully.

'Honestly, I was surprised when you said you were going to get married,' I say. 'It didn't seem like the sort of thing you do. You must have been really into Katya if you got down on one knee and popped the question.'

'Well, yeah, I was.' He pauses and I get the impression he's trying to gauge how much more he wants to talk about this. 'But it didn't exactly happen like that.'

'How did it happen then?'

'She sort of asked me. But in a roundabout way. We were both drunk and she was talking about how her best friend had just got engaged – to a fucking *Scandinavian prince* – and she was talking about how cool it would be for us to get married too, and somehow we ended up deciding to do it, for a laugh.'

'A laugh?' I'm horrified by this.

He shrugs, but I can tell he's a bit embarrassed to admit to it. 'Yeah. It sounds pretty stupid now in the cold light of day. But she texted her friends the minute we agreed to do it so it was kind of set in stone from that point on.'

'And you were okay with that?'

Again, he shrugs. 'It felt right at the time. I mean, I loved her. And she really wanted it. So I figured, why not? It was something new to experience.'

I widen my eyes. 'Oh my God. You were going to get married because you were bored.'

'Not exactly,' he says heatedly, apparently horrified by that suggestion. But then he pauses and appears to think about it. 'Maybe there was an element of that. But I felt ready to settle down too.'

I look at him, taking in his handsome profile, still not quite able to believe we've bumped into each other again the way we have. My insides do a strange little twist.

'Why are you smiling at me like that?' he says, when he becomes aware of me staring at the side of his head and turns to face me again.

'I was just thinking it's good to see how much you've grown since university.'

'Grown *up* you mean?'

'No. Grown as a person. You're more self-aware than you were back then.'

'Yeah, well, in retrospect, us splitting up probably had something to do with that. It woke me up to the fact that not everything was under my control in the way I thought it had been.'

'Really? I had no idea. I thought you were totally cool about it.'

'Honestly, I had some regrets afterwards. But then barely a couple of weeks later you were with what's-his-chops, Prince Charmless, so I didn't get a chance to woo you back.'

I suppress a grin at this. 'Adrian. And he wasn't charmless exactly. He was just less *wild* than you.'

Kit gives a dismissive snort. 'Tame, you mean.'

'Straightforward and totally into me,' I counter.

His gaze is intent on mine now. 'I was totally into you.'

My insides fizz. 'You didn't show it,' I say.

He shrugs. 'No, well, I let my brother get in my head about not settling down too quickly. He said early twenties was a time to play the field and get as much experience as possible. Serious relationships were for later in life. At the time I hero-worshipped him and thought everything that came out of his mouth was gold. Shows what a naïve dickhead I was back then. I've never taken his advice again.'

'Huh. I had no idea you felt like that.'

'I'm not the type of guy to wear his heart on his sleeve.'

'Which is why I thought you were perfectly fine when we split up – happy even. You know, you really didn't appear to be that broken up the handful of times I saw you from across the room,' I point out. 'You always seemed like you were living your best life with all those other women you were constantly surrounded by.'

He shoots me a pained grin. 'I'm a great pretender.'

I think about this for a second. 'You know,' I say, 'I think I'm probably guilty of letting someone get in my head about our relationship too.'

He sits up on his elbows and looks at me with interest. 'Really? Who?'

'You remember Carrie who was on my course? She was chair of the Students' Union in our third year.'

'Carrie with the blonde curly hair?'

'Yep.'

'Then yes, unfortunately I do.'

I blink. 'Why unfortunately?'

'We had a bit of a thing in our first year of uni that got a bit too intense, on her part. When I ended it, she was really pissed off and started borderline stalking me. At least she always seemed to turn up wherever I went. I might have been a bit paranoid about it, but whenever I did see her, which was all the bloody time, she'd just stare daggers at me for the whole night. It got really uncomfortable and I asked her to stop. She pretended she didn't know what I was talking about and claimed I was the one stalking her by turning up at the same pub or club all the time, which definitely wasn't the case.'

'Right. Wow. I had no idea that had happened. She was always really negative about you, but I didn't know she'd had a relationship with you.'

'Well, it wasn't really a relationship. We just slept with each other a couple of times after meeting during Freshers Week. I definitely wasn't up for a serious thing so soon after starting uni and I thought she felt the same. She told me she did at the time and was fine with keeping things casual, but then she changed her mind.'

'Ah. Okay. Well, she was probably really upset when you ended things then. Rejection is rejection, no matter how you couch it.'

'Yeah. I felt bad about it afterwards. Until she started her campaign of harassment, that is.'

'Hmm. Yeah. That was *not* okay behaviour.'

'And she never told you about it?' he asks.

I shake my head. 'No. She was always just dismissive and a bit bitchy about you. And if I'm honest, I let her criticism get in my head a bit. She used to go on and on about what a player you were and how you were someone who couldn't be trusted. And that I should give you a wide berth. Now I think about it, I remember her telling me you'd treated a friend of hers really badly and left her broken. I guess she didn't want to admit it was actually her.'

He lets out a frustrated-sounding breath. 'That sounds about right.'

'I mean, I mostly ignored her when we first got together because I was having such a blast with you,' I say. 'But after a while, when I felt like things could get more serious between us – that I wanted them to, but you didn't seem to – I let what she'd said get to me.'

'I wish we'd talked more, back then,' he says with regret in his voice.

Pausing for a moment, I weigh up whether I should admit to

the thing that's been rattling round my brain for a while now. I decide I may as well tell him everything. I've got nothing to lose.

'Okay, this is embarrassing,' I say, 'but in all honesty, I was a bit scared about the way you made me feel when we were together.'

'How so?'

'Out of control of my feelings. I used to think about you all the time when we weren't together. In an obsessive sort of way. It didn't feel healthy to be so infatuated with someone. Especially because you didn't seem to feel the same way. It felt unbalanced, like you had some kind of dangerous hold over me. I hated that.'

'Why didn't you tell me this at the time?'

'Because it would have given you even more power over me,' I say with a tight grin.

'Or I could have reassured you and altered my behaviour so you didn't feel so spun out.'

'But would you have done? It didn't seem like it at the time. You were having too much fun being wild and free. You didn't want me tying you down.'

'No. I wanted to do the tying down,' he says with a twinkle in his eye.

'Trust you to bring this back to sex,' I joke, feeling my whole body heat in response.

He lifts his hands in mock-apology. 'In all seriousness, I guess you're right. I probably would have freaked out.'

'So it was all down to bad timing for us. We needed very different things at the time.'

'I guess that's the crux of it, yeah.' He's looking at me intently now, his dark gaze searching my face.

'So there are no hard feelings?' I ask.

'I always have *hard* feelings around you.' The corner of his mouth lifts in a smirk. 'And I was a bit cut up at the time, yeah, but I got over it.'

I find I have to force myself to smile at that.

So he's totally over me now? The words slide like ice down my back.

I mean, I'm glad to hear he's not holding on to any kind of grudge about our past, but I'm also strangely upset to hear he doesn't have any feelings for me any more. I know that's selfish, I'm not in any state to start a serious relationship with him – *and that was never the deal* – but deep down I have to admit I like the idea of him still caring about me.

Instead of admitting to that, I dip my head, look up at him from under my lashes and say, 'Well, if there's any lingering need for closure in your mind, you'd be well within your rights to demand some sort of penance from me.'

His eyes spark with interest. 'Yeah?'

I swallow hard, my body suddenly hot and needy at the thought of us role-playing a scene where he makes me 'pay' for any hurt I've caused him. 'Yeah.'

'So, what are you saying? That you want me to punish you for it?' He quirks a suggestive eyebrow.

I raise an amused eyebrow back, relieved that we're back to our jokey banter. It was all feeling a bit too emotionally heavy there for a second and I don't have the bandwidth to deal with any more angst today. 'I guess you could. If you wanted.'

His grin is wide and genuine now. 'I'd be okay with that,' he says in a low, gruff voice. 'You still have the same preferences as before?'

'Yep.'

'Any constraints?'

'Hopefully,' I say, happy to be teasing him again now.

I shove any lingering thoughts of deeper emotions right out of my head.

'Funny,' he quips. 'I mean, are there any new boundaries I should know about? Anything you're not keen on?'

'Nope. Same, same.'

He nods. 'Okay.'

Then it's like someone's flicked a switch in his head because his expression turns serious and he gets up from the bed and turns to stand in front of me, a look of deep contemplation on his face, as if he's assessing my body from head to toe, deciding what he's going to do to me.

I immediately flush with excited heat.

It's like my body remembers the cues, without me having to consciously think about it.

Not that I'm *not* thinking about it.

Because I am.

I'm *so* into the idea of this. I need it.

'Wait here until I tell you what I want you to do.'

I do as he says, my pulse starting to race as I watch him walk away from where I'm sitting, looking around the room for something.

I have no other option. There's no way I could make myself get up and leave right now anyway. I want to continue this sex-only fling with him too much.

And I want *him*.

I remember very clearly now why I was so befuddled by him five years ago, despite the sensible side of my brain telling me he wasn't someone I should risk my heart on.

It's still nudging me. Saying this all seems too good to be true.

But I'm not here for reality, I remind myself.

This is pure escapism.

12

CHLOE

Kit returns to where I'm sitting on the edge of the bed, my knees jiggling nervously, with what appears to be the silk belts from two kimono-style dressing gowns that were provided with the room and a pair of slippers with rubber soles.

My skin tingles all over in anticipation of what's about to go down here.

'I'm going to have to improvise, Dasher. Which, luckily for you, I'm very good at.'

I nod and swallow hard.

'Go into the bathroom and take your clothes off, then come back out here and stand by the bed,' he instructs me calmly.

I get up and do what he says, leaving my clothes folded up neatly on the tallboy in there. Before leaving the bathroom, I stare at myself in the mirror for five full seconds, thinking myself into a submissive role. My heart is racing with a mixture of excitement and nerves. It's been so long since I did this, but from the way my body and mind are automatically responding in such a positive way, that's not going to be a problem.

I walk back on shaky legs to where he's waiting for me.

'Stand and face me,' he says.

I do it.

He takes a pace away from me and spends a few moments looking at me, from the top of my head to my toes. It's a thorough examination and my skin hums with awareness, almost as if I can feel his gaze physically touching me.

'Beautiful,' he says when his eyes finally meet mine again.

'Thank you.'

'Did I say you could speak?' he says, raising one chastising eyebrow at me.

I shake my head.

'Hold out your right hand,' he tells me.

I do as he says and he picks up one of the slippers he's left on the bed and slaps it against my palm, just hard enough to leave a delicious sting in its wake. I feel reverberations of the sensation deep inside my pussy.

He puts down the slipper and picks up one of the belts.

'Hold your wrists out together in front of you,' he says, nodding to my hands.

Again, I do as he says, my heart skittering.

He winds the belt around my wrists so I can't move my arms apart now, though not so tightly there's any danger of it cutting off my circulation.

He's standing so close to me I can feel heat coming in waves from his body and feathering against my naked skin. And his delicious, unique scent is in the air all around me, winding through my senses and rooting me into the scene.

Everything is heightened, in the most brilliantly intense way.

At this moment, in my mind, it's just me and him in this world. No-one else exists.

It's such a freeing feeling.

Tucking one end of the belt in between my palms, so I can

release myself if the restraint starts getting too tight, he then picks up the loose end and tugs on it, leading me to the head of the bed.

'Lie down with your arms stretched above you,' he says.

I do this, forcing myself not to watch what he's doing as I feel the belt jerk gently as he ties the end of it to part of the bedhead.

'Ready to take your punishment?' he says, though I know it's not really a question. It's a statement of intent.

I nod anyway, playing the game.

Picking up the slipper again, he walks to the middle of the bed then grasps both of my ankles in his large hand and lifts them, so I'm forced to bend in the middle, exposing my arse to him.

'Right, let's get you warmed up,' he says and starts to tap my left buttock with the slipper, gently at first, but getting increasingly harder as he tests my reaction to his strokes. I count twelve strokes before he moves on to do the same to my right buttock.

None of this hurts very much, but I still feel a glowing heat and a delicious hum of sensation on my skin where the slipper made contact.

Kit then puts down the slipper and, still holding on to my ankles with one hand, gently rubs his other hand over the area of skin that's just been targeted.

'Hmm. Starting to look a very nice colour,' he says, then picks up the slipper and does the same thing again, this time with more weight behind the strokes.

This sting is more intense now, but still incredibly pleasurable, and when he runs his hand over my skin this time, it prickles under his touch.

'I think you can take one more round,' Kit says, already picking up the slipper to administer it.

This time, the pain is right on the edge of pleasure, but the moment he finishes his last stroke, I feel endorphins rushing to the site and all the way through my body, sending my mind spinning into an ecstatic high.

I let out a long rush of breath.

'You know why you're being punished?' I hear Kit ask through my fog of desire.

'Yes,' I whisper.

'And you agree that you deserve it?'

'Yes. I do.'

'Good. Then you get a reward for doing what you've been told,' he says, then lowers my legs back to the mattress and, moving to the end of the bed, kneels down on it and grasps both ankles again, pulling my legs apart so they're now spread in front of him.

My body gives a shiver of excited anticipation as he firmly slides his hands up my calves, then my thighs, pushing them even further apart.

Then he moves closer and lowers his head, hovering his mouth above my pussy, the heat from his breath radiating over me and making me squirm with longing for him to dip even lower.

I hear him chuckle as he feels my needy body writhe beneath him. 'Always so eager for my mouth, aren't you?'

His words add another wave of stuttered sensation against my clit and I let out a strangled sort of moan in the back of my throat.

But still he makes me wait, for what feels like minutes but is probably only seconds.

I'm aware of my breathing speeding up as I wait, till I'm panting for his touch.

So the moment I feel his tongue slip firmly between my folds and up and over my clit I nearly come, unconsciously pushing my pelvis higher in the hope to feel his tongue on me there again.

As if sensing how close I am already, Kit tips his head up to look me directly in the eyes.

'No, no, no, Dasher. You don't get to come yet. Not till I'm finished with you and you've taken everything I'm going to give you. This is a punishment, remember?'

Letting out a groan of frustration, I nod my head.

Then he moves back off the bed and stands up. After pushing my legs together, he grabs my ankles again and the slipper and does the whole thing all over again.

Then again.

By the time he's hovering his mouth over my pussy for the third time, I'm almost frantic with the need to come. I'm so wet I can feel it all over the tops of my thighs.

After allowing me one long, firm, torturous press of his tongue against my clit, he leaves me twisting my hips with frustration and gets off the bed again.

'Okay, I'm going to fuck you now. And you're going to take it until I'm satisfied you've paid your dues,' he says, one eyebrow quirked, as if asking me if I understand.

I just nod. I know my place and that I'm not going to get what I want – what I *need* – if I make a false move here and speak.

I watch in fascination as he strips off his clothes, pausing only to take a condom out of the back pocket of his jeans.

He slowly rolls it onto his beautiful, hard cock, the mere sight of this making my body shiver with longing.

The anticipation is almost too much.

I'm feverish with excitement, my skin wreathed with a mist of sweat and my nerve endings fizzy and alive.

Picking up the other silk belt, he wraps it around my ankles this time and I wonder wildly for a second how he's going to fuck me if my legs are tied together.

A moment later I find out, when he grasps my tied ankles and pulls me further down the bed, until my arms are stretched as much as they'll go and my bottom is now at the end of the mattress. Then he lifts my legs again so my pussy is fully exposed to him. Luckily the bed is a high one, putting his cock at just the right level to penetrate me.

Though he doesn't do this.

Instead, he pushes first one thick finger, then another, into my pussy, then curls them up to find my g-spot and gives it a few hard curling strokes, making my entire body twitch and writhe with the intensity of the sensation.

I'm so close. So, *so* close to coming.

But *still* he makes me wait, first stilling his movements, then withdrawing his fingers fully, leaving me panting and moaning with frustration.

'Please,' I beg, unable to keep quiet any more.

I hear him give a low laugh.

'You're not allowed to come until I say you can. Do you understand?'

I nod wildly, afraid he'll make me wait even longer if I speak again.

'Say it,' he instructs me.

'Yes. I understand,' I gasp on an out-breath.

'Good.'

Then, finally, *finally*, he lines himself up and pushes his cock inside me.

I moan with pleasure as he fills me, pushing deep, all the way to his hilt.

I have to bite down on my lip in an attempt to distract myself from the building need inside me.

Now he's told me I can't come yet it's all I can think about.

I want to. I *need* to, but I can't and I won't.

Not yet.

I *love* this kind of teasing he's subjecting me to. It's so hot. Such a powerful turn on.

And I love giving myself over to it. For someone else to take control and for me to only have to think about the instructions I'm being given and how to carry them out.

It's a wonderful holiday from all the angst and pain that's been turning through my head for the last few days.

This is all about *me* and the pleasure I'm experiencing.

All thoughts flee my head as he starts to thrust inside me, my bound ankles now resting on his left shoulder so I can see his expression of unreserved satisfaction as he fucks me hard.

Having my legs tied together means there's increased tightness in my pussy as he pushes into me, and I can see from the intense concentration on his face that he's pretty close to coming too.

He's enjoying this scene just as much as I am.

'Please, please, please,' I moan under my breath as his cock slides repeatedly past my engorged g-spot and the pressure between my legs squeezes my clit.

I'm so close, so damn close. I don't know if I can hold my orgasm off much longer.

Just as I'm about to give in and tell him this, despite the fact I know it might make him stop what he's doing and force me to wait even longer, he says, 'Okay. You can come now,' in a voice that sounds like he's right on the edge too.

I need nothing more to finally let go and allow my body the release it's been desperate for.

So I do.

I come so hard every muscle in my body seems to spasm in

ecstasy and I lose control of my voice, moaning out my relief as my senses narrow and zero-in on the overwhelming sensations rushing through me now, my entire being turning into one big ball of pleasure.

I'm only vaguely aware of Kit shouting out too as he shudders into his own release inside me.

* * *

'How are you so good at that?' I say minutes later, when we're both lying together, unbound now and staring at each other in mutual appreciation.

'Well, I'd like to say natural aptitude, but I have to put some of it down to practice I suppose. There are some things I like to spend a lot of time studying.' He grins at me and I smile back.

'So sex with Katya was good, I assume?' I say, unable to help myself. I know I shouldn't be asking things like this but I'm fascinated about his relationship with his ex.

More of that sexual jealousy raising its head, I suppose.

'Yeah. Mostly,' he says, not seeming to be bothered by my question. 'She was really serious about her career as a model though so she didn't ever want to do any impact play. She couldn't afford to have any marks on her skin.'

'Oh. Right.'

There's a tense pause where neither of us says anything for a moment. It's a bit weird, I guess, bringing the phantoms of our exes into the room with us when we've been so intimate with each other for the last half an hour.

'Did you and the ex-arsehole...?'

I quirk a smile. 'He tried.'

'Uh-oh. That sounds bad.'

'It wasn't bad, exactly. We tried it at the beginning of our relationship, but he wasn't keen. He said he hated the idea of hurting me. Even though he knew I didn't see it like that.'

'I see.'

There's a moment's pause where we both silently acknowledge that we 'see' it in the same way.

'Anyway, he said he didn't want to yuk my yum, but the way he acted about it, like it was something to be worried and a bit ashamed about, took all the fun out of it for me. He tried to get into it, but he bought these fluffy handcuffs, like you get in hen do kits, and a flogger with a big pink heart on it from one of those high street lingerie shops, which felt really lame and infantilising, and it kinda put me off. Then he barely touched me with it and had a bit of a freak out about how red my skin looked afterwards. It totally killed the mood and I never brought it up again.'

'Disappointing.'

That grin of his is so telling.

I give a stiff shrug. 'I guess our kinks just weren't really in tune.'

'Like yours and mine are?'

'I guess so,' I concede, not without a little difficulty. I feel a bit foolish now for assuming we weren't well matched all those years ago – at least not in the most important ways for me at the time.

Perhaps I was a bit quick to want to grow up and be serious back then though.

'I think, sexually, we understand each other's rhythms,' I agree. 'You seem to know exactly how to touch me and what to say to turn me to jelly.'

'Yeah, it's kind of instinctive with you.' His eyes are alive with satisfaction, but I can't begrudge him that. 'Like you say, I think our bodies are attuned or something,' he says. 'I recognise your patterns and needs.'

'A sort of muscle memory maybe?'

'Yeah. Maybe.'

We're both silent for a few moments, listening to the quiet hum of the room.

Kit breaks it by turning to look at me and saying, 'I love that you're so vocal when you're enjoying something. It's a real turn on to know what I'm doing is working for you too.'

I encircle the pillow with my arms and snuggle further into it, smiling at him. 'I'm glad.'

'And you'll tell me if you're not into something, so I can change it up?'

I'm delighted to hear he's up for more of this. My skin gives a shiver of pleasure at the thought. 'Sure,' I say nonchalantly, not wanting to seem too eager. 'But so far, I have no notes, believe me. That was perfect.'

'My ego says thanks.'

'Tell it, welcome.'

He grins then gives a decisive sort of nod.

'Okay, well, I'm going to head back to my apartment and let you sleep,' he says, rolling away from me and off the bed, then starts to pull on his clothes.

I feel a rush of disappointment that he's leaving. Not that we'd had an arrangement that he'd stay over.

This is only sex, I forcibly remind myself.

'But I'll see you tomorrow for more adventures,' he promises, as if he's sensed my emotional wobble.

'Come to the samurai training with me,' I say, before I have a chance to check myself. I'd looked at the website earlier to see if there were any spaces left in my time slot and it seems there still are.

He pauses what he's doing and looks back at me, his brow raised in contemplation. 'Okay. I could probably get into that. I've always wanted to learn how to wield a sword.'

'Like a true hero.'

'Exactly, Dasher.'

'Then I'll see you back here at nine,' I say, squashing my grin.

'Okay.' He finishes pulling down his shirt, flicking out the collar in that style-conscious way of his, and walks to the door to put on his shoes. 'Sweet dreams,' he says, blowing me a kiss before opening the door and leaving.

I start to miss him the moment he's gone.

13

KIT

I'm up bright and early the next morning and after scoffing the breakfast that's brought to my apartment, I head over to Chloe's room and tap gently on the door.

It's opened almost immediately, as if she was standing right behind it.

'Hey,' she says when she sees it's me. 'Good morning.'

'Did you sleep well?' I ask, giving her a rueful smile. I certainly did.

'Yeah. Like the dead,' she says, grinning back.

There's a strangely awkward pause where we both just gaze at each other.

Is she feeling as spun out about everything we shared last night as I am? It was a revelation to hear how our break-up had actually gone down for her after being forced to make assumptions about it for the last few years. It was helpful to hear her side of the story, and I think it might have healed something inside me that's felt fractured since then.

But hey, no point in digging any deeper into what's going on here. It's a weird time all round for both of us and this is just meant to be a fun interlude, not a deep dive into something more serious.

'So,' she says, breaking the slightly tense atmosphere, 'You ready to become a samurai master?'

'Always,' I say earnestly.

I'm actually really excited about this activity. It sounds cool as fuck.

'Then let's go,' she says, following me out and pulling the door closed behind her, then leading the way down the corridor towards reception.

'I'll call my driver and get him to come and pick us up,' I say as we near the desk.

'Actually, I was thinking we'd take the tram in,' she says, before I can pull my phone out of my pocket.

'Really? You sure?' I say, not convinced I want to cram onto a tram with a load of strangers right now. Despite my reservations, I'm enjoying this intimacy we're sharing at the moment. It's almost like we're a real couple.

'Yes, I'm sure,' she says with confidence. 'We're here to experience the culture of the city, right? You're going to miss a tonne of it if you keep getting exclusive transport everywhere,' she points out, but with no malice. It's just stated as a fact.

Straightforward as always.

* * *

The tram is busy. So busy I find myself pressed up hard against Chloe.

As I breathe in her familiar scent and feel the heat from her body warming mine, I decide it's not so bad travelling this way.

She gives a wriggle against me and I wonder if she's having the same punch of awareness I am.

A sudden wave of happiness hits me as I think about how great it is to be spending this time with her. I feel like we've both matured enough now to be able to just be friends with bennies. Though, if I'm being honest, it feels like we *could* be more than that.

I'm bummed about the timing of bumping into her. It's taken out any possibility of this turning into anything more right now. And if not now, then when?

Once we're both back doing what we usually do, day to day, there's a good chance we won't have an opportunity to see each other again. Unless we make one.

And she's not suggested she'd be interested in doing that. In fact, I really should wind my neck in here. She's made it very clear what she wants from me.

Just sex.

I should think myself lucky, I guess, having the opportunity for something so uncomplicated and fun, but for some reason I'm not feeling it.

My phone buzzes in my pocket and I shift around, feeling like I'm in a straightjacket in the press of tourists all heading into the city, until I'm able to slide it out and look at the banner on the screen. I hope it's Elliot finally getting back to me.

My heart skips when I see it's a message from Katya, which starts with:

> Hey, I hope I haven't caught you at a tricky
> time. I need to speak to you urgently. I'm—

And the rest is cut off. I'm going to have to open my messaging app to read the rest.

Which I don't want to do when I'm standing so close to Chloe.

What the hell does Katya want from me now?

I half want to know and half don't.

It could be anything completing that sentence. Myriad possibilities tick through my head, each one more extreme than the last.

Pregnant is one that keeps flashing alarmingly through my mind.

But surely not.

We had a pregnancy scare at one point when she was fasting for a job and her low weight affected her cycle and caused her to miss a period, but we'd been careful since then. At least, I thought we had been. The last thing she'd wanted was to have a baby while she was focused on getting her career off the ground. So surely it can't be that?

Knowing Katya, it's more likely she's bored and just trying to get my attention and it'll actually be something pretty mundane. Or she's trying to make the guy she got back together with jealous or something. That's quite likely too. She loves to play power games.

That's what I'm going to go with.

I'll look at it properly later. I don't want to ruin this trip with Chloe by dealing with it right now.

I take a breath to try and calm my racing heart.

As if sensing my tension, she looks up at me.

'Everything okay?' she asks.

'Err, yeah. It's nothing,' I say, feeling my face heat. I don't want to bullshit her, but I also don't want to drag her into whatever this is about either.

The last thing I want is for Chloe to think I'm more interested in hearing what Katya has to say than spending time with her.

I don't want to mess with what we've got going right now.

Trouble is, I know if I don't read the message it's going to keep playing on my mind and distract me.

But now is definitely not the time to deal with whatever's going on.

Shoving the phone back into my pocket, I flash Chloe what I hope looks like a reassuring smile.

'All good,' I say.

* * *

Chloe

The dojo where we're due to do our samurai training is situated off one of the main shopping streets, its entrance tucked down some steps between a noodle bar and a souvenir shop.

We tentatively descend the steps, not quite sure what to expect.

Is a samurai warrior going to jump out at us, sword brandished and eyes alight with danger?

But no. We're actually greeted by a very smiley greeter, who – once we've removed our shoes – politely instructs us to take a stool with the other participants, who are lined up in a row along the back wall.

Moments after sitting, we're fitted with our black keikogi outfits to train in, which are made of very thick, heavy cotton, the weight of which immediately makes me take the whole thing much more seriously.

The ceremony of it all clearly demands respect and focus, and I turn to see Kit also has a sombre expression on his face as he ties the belt around his waist.

When he notices me looking at him though, he gives me a covert wink, which makes my insides fizz.

Turning away before he can see my cheeks heating, I gaze around me, taking in the small shrine above the door and all the certificates and trophies proudly displayed around the walls of the dojo.

'This is a real dojo you are training in,' the sensei says, as if noticing my interest.

At least this is what I come to understand he's saying, once it's translated by his assistant, who appears to be from somewhere in the north of England, judging by his accent.

This surprising incongruity makes me grin, and I glance at Kit to see he's smiling back at me.

I love that we're on the same page with things that amuse us.

The two instructors take us through all the safety protocols and some of the history of the Samurai warriors, which is fascinating.

Kit certainly seems rapt by it all. I don't think I've ever seen him sit so still for so long.

I experience another burst of warmth towards him. It feels strange to have been so wary about being around him again when in actual fact, bumping into him has been one of the best things to happen to me in quite some time.

I decide not to examine that thought too closely right now and force myself to focus back on what the instructor is telling us.

We're then taken through some sword-wielding moves and I'm relieved to find we're given blunt swords to practise with.

The moves are graceful, a bit like a dance, and once each of us in the group have mastered them, the previously stern and sombre sensei breaks into a wide, eye-glittery smile and giggles, then gives us each a high five.

It's the most charming thing I've experienced in a very long time and makes me reflect again on how easily I fall back on my assumptions about people. Only when I give them a chance to prove me wrong do I discover the true them. I really should work on that.

My thoughts are interrupted by the sensei proclaiming he's happy with the fluidity of our sequences and he, now serious again, tells us we are about to wield a real – and extremely sharp – samurai sword.

The whole group gasps in appreciation when he brings it out and proudly shows it to us.

It's a thing of beauty, the suggestion of its potential viciousness an unsettling counterpoint to its elegant craftsmanship.

My palms grow sweaty just looking at it.

A rolled bamboo mat is placed on its end on a pedestal and the sensei goes through the technique of how to slice the sword in a diagonal motion to first cut the top of the mat clean off, then how to cut through the middle of it, reducing it to just a stub.

He expertly demonstrates this in one fluid movement, sending the two severed pieces of the mat to the floor in what feels like one second flat.

I swallow hard, intimidated by the task ahead, but determined to do it well. Thankfully, the sensei then instructs us that we should just make one cut at a time as we're beginners, which is a massive relief.

Kit goes before me and I marvel at how focused he is on getting this right. He's always been this way, at least ever since I've known him. I'm sure it's something to do with him being the youngest sibling and having been ridiculed by his brother and sister – particularly his brother – when anything he did was deemed to be less than exceptional.

I remember lying in bed with him, back in our uni days, early on in our fling, when he'd drunkenly told me about the tricky relationship he had with his family, after I'd asked him about his background. They expected so much from him and he'd never felt like he matched up to their expectations.

It had been one of the only times we'd talked about anything serious. He'd not gone back to the subject again and I got the impression he didn't usually talk about his family's dynamics.

I bet they think about him differently now though, now he's a billionaire.

That has to have gone some way towards pacifying his need to always be better and cooler than the next person.

Though perhaps not *all* the way.

He still seems to have a need to make up for the praise and respect he clearly feels he missed out on growing up, if his relationship with Katya is anything to go by.

As I watch him cut the bamboo in exactly the right place he was instructed to, and see the flash of relief on his face, my heart turns over.

I have a sudden realisation about how hard it must be for him when his relationships don't work out. It must amplify that chasm of longing to feel special that echoes inside him.

I'm brought back to the present when Kit turns to give me a smile of such satisfaction a tingle of pleasure makes its way from deep in the base of my spine up to my scalp.

He's happy – at least, in this moment he is – and it's wonderful to see it.

After receiving his high five from the sensei, he walks back to his stool and raises his hand to me too. I meet it with my own.

'Thanks for bringing me here,' he murmurs, his voice suffused with delight as he looks deep into my eyes.

I open my mouth to reply, to tell him it's my absolute pleasure – which it really has been – but before I can say anything, the sensei calls for me to come and cut my own bamboo mat.

Determined not to let myself down in front of Kit and the crowd of onlookers, I step up, check my understanding of the moves, then take a breath and guide my limbs to perform them, hoping to goodness I don't miss my target.

Even though my cuts aren't as neat as Kit's, relief trickles through me as I see the bamboo fall to the floor and I receive my own high five from the sensei.

Kit grins at me as I walk back to my stool and take my seat next to him, my legs still a little shaky with nerves.

'Nice one, Dasher. As elegant as ever,' he says, his eyes alive with approval.

In that moment I realise I like him.

Really like him.

Stunned by this unnerving insight, I quickly squash the feeling down and give him a tight smile.

'A new skill to add to our inventory,' I joke, not able to meet his eyes again in case he sees in them the very thing I don't want him to see.

14

KIT

'So, what's next?' I ask, still buzzed from wielding that incredible sword and eager to keep the joy alive as we walk up the steps from the dojo and back onto the bustling shopping street.

'Cat café?' Chloe says with an expectant lift of her eyebrow.

I try to work out if she's serious and decide from the eagerness I see flickering in her expression that she is.

I frown. 'That's not exactly what I had in mind.'

'It's actually more of an animal café. So not just cats,' she says, adopting a persuasive tone now.

'Really? What, like a zoo?' I ask, horrified by the idea. I didn't come all the way to Japan to do things an eight-year-old me would have enjoyed. Not that my brother ever let me enjoy being eight. He was always so dismissive about anything age-appropriate that I liked.

She laughs. 'I don't think there'll be anything dangerous to humans there, no. Just different types of fluffy pets.'

I laugh off my unease, but I can see from the look in her eyes that she really wants to do this. And I'm grateful to her for inviting me to come along today – the samurai training was a blast and not something I would have experienced if it wasn't for her – so I say, 'Okay then. I'll come for the ride, but I'll just sit in the corner and drink coffee, if it's all the same to you. I'm not a massive fan of petting animals.'

'Suit yourself,' she says, shrugging one shoulder in a gesture that clearly says, *if you want to pretend to be cool that's fine by me, but I know you better than that.*

I catch the corner of her mouth lift in a gratified smile and warmth pools in my chest.

* * *

'Here it is,' she says, fifteen minutes later, after we've dodged through the crowds heading towards one of the famous temples, which is set in beautiful parkland opposite the café. She points at a set of stairs that lead up to a small shopping mall. A lot of the shops here seem to be arranged on top of each other. I guess it makes economic sense, but it's strange, as a Brit, to see them stacked so high so often.

I follow her up a couple of floors until we come to a sign showing a wide-eyed kitten with a pink bow tied around its neck, looking like the mother of all innocent internet thirst traps.

Pulling open the glass door next to it, she walks into the reception area where you're expected to take off your shoes and stow them in a pigeonhole.

Once we've both done this, she goes to speak to the friendly receptionist who sets us up with treats for the animals as well as a space in a cabinet where we can safely stow any drinks we buy while we're there.

Chloe makes a beeline for a small two-person sofa, and the moment she's seated and has opened what looks like a small bowl of chocolate – which I'm pretty sure it isn't – she's swamped by about seven cats and kittens, all vying for a lick of the loaded spoon she's holding out towards them.

I can't help but laugh as they begin to climb all over her, rubbing their cheeks against her arms and body and gazing up at her with their wide adoring eyes, all competing for her attention and love.

Clever pusses.

I'm almost jealous of the rapt way she's gazing back at them, her voice a low, seductive purr as she gently admonishes them for pushing each other out of the way.

Her smile is the widest I've seen it since I first bumped into her again, here in Kyoto.

I've definitely been a facilitator of intense pleasure for her here too, mostly when she's been in bed with me, I'm satisfied to note. Though she's seemed to enjoy my company out of bed too.

As I have hers.

In fact, I don't think I've laughed so much with someone for quite some time. Life all got a bit serious there for a while and it's such a balm to actually have some fun again for a change. I've definitely grown up a lot in the intervening years, but Chloe seems to have brought back the adventurous side in me.

I'm starting to realise how much I've missed it.

As if sensing I'm thinking about her, she looks up and catches my eye, grinning as a tiny and very furry grey kitten makes itself comfortable on her lap, seemingly sated now from the brown gloopy treat it's been eating. It stretches out its entire length along the middle of her lap, its tiny chin propped on her right knee.

She puts down the bowl and spoon, which appear to have been licked clean now, and the rest of the cats wander off, spotting a new couple of people coming into the café with their own smorgasbord of treats clutched in their hands.

'How's your pussy?' I ask with a grin, nodding down at the kitten in her lap.

She smirks back. 'Purring.'

'Can I have a stroke?' I ask, all mock innocence.

This time she laughs. 'Sure. Take a seat and go for your life.'

I sit next to her on the sofa and turn to make a joke about the heat between her legs, but before I know what's happening, one of the people who work there, looking after the animals, puts a ferret on my lap.

A goddamn *ferret*!

I stare at it in horror, barely able to believe it's really there. It's like something from one of my nightmares, where something is intent on taking a bite out of my dick.

Don't ask me to explain those dreams. My therapist's had a good go at getting me to 'unpick' where that fear has come from, but I still have no earthly clue.

Though isn't every guy mortally afraid of castration?

'Jesus,' I whisper, sickening heat swamping me as I lean as far back as I can from the offending creature that's now walking around in my lap, trying to get more comfortable.

'You don't want it?' the café employee asks, sounding not only surprised, but a bit miffed.

'No. Take it away. Please,' I manage to grind out through gritted teeth.

Thankfully, she does as I ask, scooping the long, pale, furry creature, *with razor sharp teeth*, away from my crotch, then gives it a consoling cuddle before putting it back in a cat basket.

My heart is racing and my palms are sweaty with the lingering fear, so it takes me a moment to realise that Chloe is frowning at me in concern.

'You okay?' she asks. 'You've gone a bit pale.'

'Is it any wonder?' I gasp out. 'Those things have needles for teeth and they love to burrow their way inside trouser legs!'

I can tell she's trying not to smile and I swallow hard, my throat dry and my frown deepening as humiliation creeps over me.

This is not how I hoped this little interlude would go. I want Chloe to see me as a strong, capable human being, not some weak, anxiety-ridden kid.

'Hey,' she says, lifting her hand and cupping my jaw. Her touch is like a balm, and I feel myself start to relax as I look into her eyes and see only compassion there. 'It's okay to feel afraid. No-one's judging you, especially not me.' And she leans in and kisses me firmly on the lips, as if wanting to prove she means it.

A sense of relief floods through me and I lean into the kiss, grateful for the distraction from my angst.

When she pulls away, her eyes are shining and she gives me a gentle smile, her expression full of warmth.

That's new. Up until now, all I've had are playful smiles from her, but this one feels more genuine, like she actually cares about me.

Not wanting to 'unpick' that either right now, I stand up from the sofa and clap my hands gently together.

I'm feeling pretty fucking spun-out right now.

'Okay. I'm going to find my drink. I'll be back in a minute,' I say, not waiting for her reply before I head off to the cabinet to soothe my now rather rough-feeling throat with the coffee I ordered when we first came in, which has been deposited on our shelf.

I knock back the entire drink, grateful for a short reprieve from what felt like a significant moment just now. I know we're only hanging out with each other while we're both here in

Kyoto, but I'm already beginning to wonder how I'm going to deal with it when it's time for us to say goodbye to each other.

I'm distracted from that unsettling thought by one of the other employees approaching me with a friendly smile and what looks like a cat's toy. It's a long wooden stick, with a rainbow-coloured piece of furry material attached to it, which I guess is meant to represent an animal's tail.

I stare at it quizzically for a moment, until she points towards a metre-high plastic partition a few feet away from us, which runs the width of the room and has a small gate in the middle of it.

Looking over the makeshift fence, I see two small creatures wrestling with each other, their tails whipping around as they tumble over and over along the floor.

They're meerkats. Bloody *meerkats*.

They're hilarious though, and look like a couple of rambunctious siblings, larking around together. As I watch, they separate, then start to chase each other's tails, playfully trying to bite the other's, though clearly not with any intent to hurt.

It makes me think about how my brother and I used to play-fight when I was eight and he was twelve. Though ours had been much less about play and more about dominance. Of which he usually got the upper hand, being older and bigger than me. Not to mention more competitive.

Not much has changed since we grew up. It was one of the best days of my life when I got to tell him I'd become a billionaire – something he could never dream of becoming, even as a top-flight barrister.

His reserved congratulations and gritted-teeth smile felt like a victory at the time, but since then I've heard from him less and less. I guess because the money's become a bit of a barrier between us. I finally beat him at something and he hates it.

I'm distracted from my thoughts by the employee waving the cat toy at me again and insistently nodding towards the meerkats.

So I take it from her and let myself in through the gate, moving slowly over to where the two of them have now separated so one of them can sit on its hind legs and look around him for any danger, keeping the both of them safe, I guess.

I get a strange little flutter in my chest as I see how focused these guys are on looking out for each other.

It's not something me and my siblings have ever been any good at.

I've always just taken care of myself.

Dutifully, I bounce the colourful tail near the meerkat that's not on guard duty and he takes up the challenge immediately, running in circles and almost cartwheeling whilst trying to grab hold of it with his paws and teeth.

I find myself starting to laugh as his brother joins him and we all play around for a bit, enjoying each other's company in a way I never have before with animals.

Perhaps I should get myself a couple of meerkats for housemates once I get home.

Joke.

But in all seriousness, it's going to feel pretty empty in my house with just me rattling around in it until it's finally sold.

Unless I don't go home.

Perhaps I should keep travelling round the world for the rest of my life?

But I know, as soon as I've thought this, that I wouldn't want to do it alone.

My eyes are drawn to Chloe, who's still pinned to the sofa by the sleeping kitten.

She glances up, as if sensing I'm looking for her, and smiles.

My heart turns over.

Jesus.

I really need to pull myself together, or I'm going to fuck things – and myself – up.

We're just having fun. This isn't going to turn into anything serious. She's still too raw after her split with that arsehole.

'You look like you're having fun, counter to all your "I'm too cool for this" instincts,' she calls over to me.

'Yeah, okay, Dasher. You win, this is fun,' I admit, flashing her a grin.

Her laugh is warm and full-throated.

'I'm guessing this is the cheapest fun you've had in a while?' she says.

'Oh, I don't know,' I fire back, raising a suggestive eyebrow.

'I hope you're not calling me cheap,' she says, but there's levity to her voice.

I hold up my hand. 'I wouldn't dare. Not now you know how to cut me in two with a sword,' I point out.

* * *

We spend another happy hour there, having first rabbits, then a miniature pig, of all things, put in our laps to stroke.

This has to be the weirdest afternoon I've ever spent, but it's also one of the most fun.

From the looks of it, Chloe's having the same experience as I am.

Which I'm glad about.

She deserves to be happy.

And I love how she challenges me. I love her fire – but also her compassion.

If there's one thing Chloe could never be, it's dull.

Unlike her fucking stooge of an ex.

I can image being with him must have drained the life out of her, to the point where she became so institutionalised, she couldn't see how bad the relationship was for her.

Hopefully she's beginning to see it now though. Now she's had some time away from him.

With me.

When we've finally had our fill of petting the weird – and okay, wonderful – animals, we wash our hands, then pay for our session and put our shoes back on.

Leaving the café, we stroll back out onto the bustling streets of Kyoto.

'You hungry?' I ask her.

'Ravenous.'

'Want to get some food back at the hotel?'

'Yeah, sure, I'd love to.'

* * *

We don't order any food. We're too busy ripping each other's clothes off the moment we've stepped in through the door to my apartment.

There are no games this time. It's just straight need driving us. And something else too. It also feels tender and loving this time as we move together in sync, our bodies melding into each other perfectly.

We're a great fit.

Fuck, I'm going to miss this.

But is she?

I push away the question and force myself to focus on what's happening in the room right now.

The smell of her. The sounds she's making in the back of her throat as she gets close to orgasm. The feel of her legs wrapped around me. The taste of her on my lips. The sight of her beautiful face as it screws up in concentration. The grip of her fingertips against my back when she finally comes beneath me as I thrust into her.

It's not long till I'm coming too. Hard. All my senses overloaded with pleasure.

Afterwards we're both a sweaty mess, but neither of us care as we cling to each other, coming down from our respective highs.

I finally slide out of her and peel myself away from her body, rolling onto the mattress alongside her.

Both of us are still breathing fast and I turn my head to look at her at the same time she looks round at me.

We stare at each other, almost like we're surprised by how much we enjoyed that.

It just felt right.

I'm about to open my mouth to tell her how fucking great I think she is when she beats me to it by saying, 'I've only got tonight here left then I'm heading back to Tokyo via the Studio Ghibli park before I fly home.'

I blink at her, momentarily confused by the sudden change in mood. 'Oh, right. I can't believe we've been here for nearly a week already,' I say, turning away and running my hand over my hair.

'Yeah, I know. The time's gone too fast.'

The thought of her leaving is making my stomach sink.

I don't want this to end. I want her to stay here, in my arms, in my bed until the end of time.

'Hey. Wild idea,' I say, turning back to catch her eye. 'Don't go home yet. Come travelling with me for another week. Or longer, if you like. Everywhere I'll be staying I'll be paying a double room rate so it makes no difference to me. I'll also have a car to take us places so all the travel will be covered. And I'll ask my PA to call the airline and get your flight moved by a week. She's brilliant at getting those kind of things sorted and she's twiddling her thumbs at the minute while I'm holidaying here.'

My heart is racing at the idea of this. I'm excited about it.

But is she?

I'm amazed how nervous I feel, waiting for her answer.

She seems to think about this for a whole minute. 'Well, I have to admit, these last few days with you have been a hell of a lot more fun than spending them either alone or in therapy bawling my eyes out, going over and over what I did wrong in order for my relationship to implode like it did,' she says with a wry smile.

'Glad to have been of service,' I manage to joke, though I'm more intent on knowing what her answer to my suggestion is.

But instead of saying 'Yes, great idea, I'd love to', she goes quiet again and stares, unblinking, up at the ceiling.

'So don't go yet,' I prompt, unable to help myself. 'I think we have something good going here. Something we could explore more.'

'Lots more fun to be had?' she says quietly, but not in the excited, accepting way I'm hoping for.

I can't work out where her head's at.

She's gone frustratingly insular all of a sudden.

'So, what do you say? Will you stay on a bit longer?' I ask, unable to stop myself from pushing it.

Before she can answer, my phone pings with a message.

The usually upbeat note sounds ominous in the quiet room. I have a horrible feeling I know who this is going to be from, and my pulse picks up as anxiety rises through my chest.

I frown at the phone but don't move to pick it up.

'Go ahead, check your message. Don't mind me,' Chloe says, her voice tinged with concern, seeming to sense the sudden tension that's taken over my body.

I reach across for it with a thudding heart and glance at the banner, hoping I'm wrong.

I'm not. It's another message from Katya.

> Kit, please don't ignore me. I have something
> really important to discuss with you. I'm—

Again, the rest of the banner is cut off.

Once again, the word *pregnant* flashes through my mind.

Jeez, please no. Not when things have the potential right now to go further with Chloe.

In a sudden moment of clarity, it hits me that I definitely wouldn't want to hear from Katya that she's pregnant, but I wouldn't mind at all if it was Chloe telling me that. In fact, I'd probably welcome it. It would be an adventure with her – of the best kind. Because she's the best kind of person.

And I think now that fate pushed us back together for a reason.

Deciding not to look at the rest of the message, I dump my phone back on the nightstand, but Chloe is obviously suspicious about my behaviour because she looks at me quizzically.

'Are you sure everything's okay?' she asks.

'Yeah, fine.' I reach for her and slide my hand into her hair, then lean in and kiss her hard on the mouth, but she stiffens under my touch.

My heart plummets.

Something's changed.

15
CHLOE

Kit's hiding something. I'm sure of it.

There was an inflection in his voice when he said everything was fine, which doesn't sit right with me.

He'd done it on the tram on the way into the city too, but I'd pushed my concerns aside then, not wanting to spoil our trip by questioning him about it.

This feeling of unease takes me straight back to the way Adrian was acting around me in the days before the wedding was due to take place. I'd put it down to his nerves about getting married, or the thought of having to stand up in front of all the people we'd invited and being the centre of attention, which he's never enjoyed – to my subsequent regret.

If only I'd pressed him to tell me what was wrong at the time, we could have avoided some of the traumatic humiliation on the day.

Because of this experience, I seem to be hyper aware now of inconsistencies in behaviour, and Kit's body language is giving off strong red flag signals.

I try to push my concerns away. It's none of my business who's messaging him. It's not like he's my partner or anything.

And what I felt for him for a second in the dojo was just the adrenaline of wielding that sword, I'm sure of it. And in the animal café, when he showed his more vulnerable side for once and I felt a strange rush of intense affection for him, it was just because I was in a happy place with a tiny warm kitten on my knee.

I think, in both cases, all those feelings just got muddled together.

That has to have been it.

In fact it's crazy that I'm even contemplating staying on longer with him. We're both very freshly out of relationships – serious ones – so it'd be ridiculous to think this is more than just a rebound. A cleansing. A revenge on Adrian and Katya for hurting us.

Having sex with Kit is one thing, but restarting our old relationship is a totally different beast.

One I'm much too frightened to face right now.

'Who's messaging you?' I blurt, unable to stop myself.

I know it's going to be bad news – or news I don't want to hear anyway – I can sense it.

My stomach feels like it's got rocks in it and a prickly panic creeps through my chest as I wait for him to tell me.

He sighs and rubs his hand over his face, like he feels I've backed him into a corner. 'Katya.'

I sit up and wrap my arms around my middle, my entire being suddenly on high alert. 'Oh?'

'Yeah, I'm ignoring them,' he says, waving his hand in the direction of the phone, like it means nothing to him.

But I can tell from the expression on his face that he's bluffing. It does mean something.

I'm not buying this nonchalant act.

'Go ahead and read them. Don't mind me. In fact' – I shuffle to the edge of the bed, aware that my heart is racing, and go to stand up – 'I should probably get back to my own room and give you some space.'

'You don't need to do that,' he says, but his voice still sounds strange.

'It's fine. Probably best that I do,' I say tightly, grabbing my clothes and starting to pull them on with fumbling fingers.

'Look, I just need to check what it says. I could only read the beginning of it and it's been playing on my mind.'

'Sure. Go ahead,' I say, not looking at him. I don't want him to see my torment in my face.

'Just, wait a second. Don't leave. Please,' he says, his tone beseeching.

This stops me in my tracks. I think he really does want me to stay. I decide to give him the benefit of the doubt.

Sitting on the edge of the bed, I twist my fingers together in my lap.

Kit reaches for his phone again and I watch as his gaze dances across the screen. He lets out a rush of breath, then I see a smile flash across his face. Clearly it's good news. For him.

'Everything okay?' I ask, unable to help myself.

'Yeah. Fine. It's just – she's coming here to the hotel to see me.' He pulls a frustrated face now, but I can tell he's trying to hide how buzzed he actually is by the idea of this. That there might still be hope for them getting back together, I guess.

Clearly it's not over between them.

Which makes sense, I suppose. She's much more his speed than me. Better suited to his billionaire lifestyle than I am, with my cat cafés and cheap travel choices.

Katya fits right into his world, without him having to adapt in any way.

And anyway, the last thing I need right now is more complication in my life.

This thought cements my decision to leave.

'Okay, then I really should go,' I say, standing up from the bed. 'I don't want to be a third wheel.'

'You really don't need to—'

'Yeah, I do. You should see her if she's making the effort to come all the way here to see you.' I take a shaky breath. 'You're obviously still in love with her and it'd be wrong for me to get in the way of you two getting back together.'

He goes to speak but I talk over him. 'I can't stay longer anyway. I have to get back to work. They need me there,' I say stiffly. 'And this was never meant to be anything more than a bit of fun, right?'

He rubs a hand over his hair. 'Err, yeah. I suppose so.'

'So let's call it finished now, before we get confused about what it is we're doing here.'

I can feel him staring at me as I pull on the rest of my clothes.

This wasn't supposed to be a *thing* with Kit. It's just a distraction, a balm.

I can't afford to allow myself to catch any feelings. I'll only get hurt. Again.

It's too soon for me to get into anything serious again anyway. I need to give myself some room to breathe before I launch into something new with someone else.

'Can we talk about this for a second?' Kit says, his voice laden with frustration.

Panic starts to rise again in my stomach. I can't deal with this right now.

'I can't spend more time with someone who's always looking over my shoulder for someone better anyway,' I bite out.

He looks affronted by that 'What? I wouldn't do that.'

'You used to.'

'I used to be a complete prick, yes, I admit it. But I'm not any more. I learnt my lesson about that when we split up.'

'Did you though? How can I trust that?' I try to make this sound persuasive, but I'm way off the mark. I actually sound defensive. Argumentative.

Kit lifts his arms in an open shrug, looking frustrated now. 'I don't know. That's something you're going to have to figure out for yourself.'

'Yeah, well, I don't have the bandwidth to do that right now,' I say with a mixture of frustration and sadness.

Finally seeming to recognise my torment, he lets out a low breath and relaxes his posture, holding up both hands in acceptance.

'Okay. Fine. If that's how you feel then perhaps you should go.' He leans back against the headboard and tips his face to the ceiling. 'I guess we had our fun.' When he looks back at me he's replaced his scowl with a nonchalant smile. 'And as a bonus, I got my closure after our split and you got your revenge on What's-his-chops by having amazing sex with your ex – yours truly – that he hates because I'm better at it than him. I call that a win-win.'

And there we have it – confirmation of what this has all really been about: a salve to Kit's pride.

I force myself to give him a smile of acknowledgement, then turn away and start walking to the door on legs that feel like they've lost all their nerves.

'Chloe,' he says loudly behind me.

I stop in my tracks, swallow past a lump in my throat and turn back to face him.

I think that's the first time he's called me by my first name, and it's had a strange effect on me.

He holds out his hand. 'Give me your phone, I'll put my number into it. In case you ever feel like shooting the breeze with me again.'

Shooting the breeze. You couldn't get more casual than that.

But hey, there's no reason why we can't be friendly towards each other now.

Without a word I hand my phone to him and watch while his thumbs skim over the screen.

Handing it back, he says, 'There you go. Now you've always got me in your pocket.'

I can't help but smile at that. 'You're a good guy, Kit. Deep down.'

'Thanks,' he says, dryly.

'And you deserve to be happy.'

'So do you, Dasher.'

I sigh. 'I will be. I just need a bit of time to heal then I'll be as good as new.'

He gives me a smile that isn't entirely convincing. 'Well. It's been a blast.'

'Yeah, it has,' I agree.

'See you around, I guess.'

'Not if I—' I grimace through a sudden melancholy that's descended. 'Yeah, I'm not going to say it.'

The corner of his mouth lifts in a grin. 'Have a good journey home.'

'Thanks, you too.' I turn to go, take a couple of steps towards the door, then spin back to face him again. 'Do you want to know what I think?'

Folding his arms, he raises both eyebrows in response. 'Hmm. I'm not sure I do, but I suspect you're going to tell me anyway.'

'You're not the sort of person who should be a billionaire. It's bad for you. Demotivating.'

'Wow. Well, I can't say I'm shocked to hear you say something like that.'

'Yeah, well. You should thank me for being honest. Clearly no-one else has had the balls to point out the truth to you. It sounds like you've surrounded yourself with *yes* people.'

'Yes, ma'am,' he jokes, his smile wide and wicked, but I could swear there's a flash of sadness behind it.

Or maybe I'm just seeing things.

'Enjoy the rest of your holiday,' I say, forcing myself to walk away from him.

'I'll give it my best shot,' he calls, right before I shut the door to his apartment behind me.

* * *

Kit

My instinct is to chase after her and tell her I don't want her to go, or that I'll come with her. But I know I can't do either of those things. She needs space. Time to heal and be able to trust again.

So do I, if I'm being honest.

The messages from Katya have shaken me up. She's asking to see me face to face and talk. Not because she's pregnant, but because she's still in love with me and wants me back. That leaving me for the ex she dumped me for was a mistake. That he's boring and never has any time for her. Or so she says.

It's more likely that now she's got what she wanted from him, she's the one who's bored and looking to get back to the cushy ride she had with me.

But there's no way I'd want to reconcile with her. It's too late. I don't love her any more.

I'm in love with Chloe.

That's extremely clear to me now.

And I'm prepared to wait for her. Because she's worth it.

As soon as I've given Katya the courtesy of a chance to say what she needs to, since she's making the effort to come all the way here, and told her we're completely finished with no chance of a reconciliation, I'm going to leave the hotel too – alone – and travel round Japan for a bit. Get my head together. Make some plans for the future.

Chloe's right of course, being mega-wealthy probably isn't good for me. It's made me take too much for granted. Made me emotionally and conscientiously lazy.

So it's time I did something about that.

* * *

The next day
Chloe

I've been wanting to visit the Studio Ghibli Park for years. Now I'm finally here all I can do is think about Kit and the fact he's not here to enjoy this with me.

As I wander around it, taking in the amazing spectacle of the life-size replicas of the houses from the films, immersive movie sets, presentations of exclusive short films and mind-boggling exhibits and carousel rides, I can't help wondering how his reconciliation with Katya went. Whether they're back together again now.

Whether he's happy.

I know I was too hard on him after he admitted to receiving those messages from her. That I unfairly lashed out at him.

I don't actually believe he lied to me in any way, but he was clearly distracted by them and I thought the best thing I could do right then was uncomplicate things for him and cut what we'd been doing off at the knees.

We'd both agreed that we weren't in the arrangement we'd struck up for the long-haul and it felt like it was important to stick to the boundaries we'd set for ourselves.

This was particularly vital because of the way I was starting to feel about him – like something had changed between us on a fundamental level. It had made me nervous. Scared even.

My head's still in too much of a mess to be able to unravel exactly what was going on there, but I know, deep down, that it was significant.

That he's important to me.

* * *

Two weeks later
Kit

I lie on my bed, listening to the ringing quiet of my hotel room, wondering what to do with myself today. I've already hit a lot of the recommended sights in Japan over the last couple of weeks and while I've been able to appreciate the magnificence of them, I've not connected with the country in the same way I did when I was with Chloe.

Or with any of the other people I've met on my travels.

I finally heard back from Elliot though, which was a massive fucking relief. Apparently he's been keeping his head down at his Vanaheim Grand hotel in Saint Lucia. Not that he gave much away about what he's been up to there and why he's been ghosting me. All I got in reply to my question about whether he's having woman trouble was:

> Yeah. It's all a bit complicated and a proper head-fuck if I'm honest. I'm okay. Kinda. Spun out. I've got some shit to work through, but it's going to be okay. Don't worry about me, dude.

So that's enigmatic of him.

Honestly, it didn't really help with my worry, but at least he's back in contact. He knows I've got his back, no matter what, so hopefully if I can be of any assistance he'll let me know.

It sounds as if Raffa's having a crisis of his own right now too, which is very unlike him. I'm poised for hearing all about this wedding of his step-brother's that he was reluctantly going to. I know he'd arranged for it to be held, gratis, at the last minute at the Vanaheim Grand in the Maldives but I don't know who he got to be his 'unsuitable' date for it. I guess I'll hear all the gory details in due course when he next gets in touch.

On the theme of people getting in touch, I pick up my phone to check whether Chloe's sent me a message yet.

Nope.

Radio silence.

So I log in to my bank accounts and stare at the long strings of numbers that usually give me such a thrill.

Nothing. They mean absolutely nothing to me right now. Just a big load of zeros.

Logging off, I toss my phone onto the bedside table and

resume my staring up at the ceiling, aware of an annoying tension in my throat.

I try to swallow past it, but it won't go away.

There's a heavy ache in my chest too.

And my eyes keep watering.

I fucking miss her.

16

ONE MONTH LATER

Chloe

It's been a tough few weeks since I got back from Japan.

I've spent a lot of time disentangling myself from the things I'd shared with Adrian and rebuilding my life into a different shape, which has been painful, but necessary.

I've needed this time to pull the ragged edges of my life back together and start to feel more whole again.

But I'm aware there's still a gap left. And that it's Kit shaped.

Every day, since I walked out on him, I've checked his social media, expecting to see pictures of him with Katya. But every day there's been no sign of her on any of his feeds. I guess she's still busy working on her new modelling campaign.

When he has posted, he's mostly put up things about a place he's visiting in Japan, looking like he's having a blast.

He's not posted for a couple of weeks now though.

It makes me wonder whether he's met someone new. He didn't seem to use social media at all when he was with me. I know. I've checked.

Yesterday, in a moment of weakness, I actually went to look up his number on my phone, just to see his name, and was confused to find it wasn't in my list of contacts. It took me a minute of scrolling up and down to find him. I knew immediately it was his number when I saw he'd chosen *Best Ex* for his pseudonym.

It was so Kit.

I burst out laughing at that, then inexplicably started to cry.

Unfortunately, I was at work at the time. Luckily my colleagues assumed my red puffy eyes were something to do with Adrian and the aborted wedding, so I'd not needed to give them an excuse.

I really am incredibly lucky to be working with such amazing people.

They'd all been so kind to me when I got back from Japan and gave me the space and unquestioning support I needed so I could get on with my job and have some sort of normalcy back in my life.

Speaking of kindness, I've thought back a lot to my time at the hotel with Kit. To the compassion he'd shown me. The patience and the warmth.

He'd helped me out repeatedly, without making any kind of deal about it. And he'd been respectful about my wants and needs without letting me walk all over him.

In fact, he'd propped me up there in all sorts of ways without complaint and hadn't once run for the hills when things got sticky and uncomfortable.

Because he has integrity.

And okay, he's not exactly the humble type, but honestly, who cares about that really? In reality, I actually like and appreciate his self-assurance. And no-one's perfect, right?

It occurred to me that the rambling list of traits and character strengths I'd outlined in the hot tub, when we'd first danced around each other at the beginning of the holiday, were there, *in him*, all along. I was just too self-centred and short-sighted to see them.

But I see them now.

And that we were good together.

Kit made me happy and encouraged me to be myself in a way that Adrian never did.

That's what I want in a partner.

Kit's what I've always wanted. I was just too naïve to realise it.

I know it now though.

But I've got a horrible feeling I might have missed my chance. My *second* chance.

Even if I have, I hope we'll always be able to be friends. If he's amenable to that. I wasn't exactly friendly towards him at the end.

I half want to know and I half don't, because I have a horrible feeling it'll hurt more to be rejected by Kit than it did by Adrian.

But if I don't get in contact with him I'll always wonder.

At the weekend I take a walk to the place I've visited a lot in the last month. A park I'd never been to before I went to Japan, but now can't seem to stay away from.

The sun is shining, so I sit down on a bench and take a couple of pictures with my phone of the magnificent scene in front of me: of the cherry trees, which in Japan are thought to represent not only the transience of life but also hope, renewal and new beginnings, the intensity of the dark red maple trees against the vibrant greens of the foliage, the waterfall cascading into a large pond of Japanese fish and even a peacock strutting past, reminding me of Kit and his pretend preening at the dinner table that first night we spent together.

The memory makes me smile.

This place was a gift from Japan to London and it seems more than fitting to be sharing pictures of it with Kit.

So I take a breath, attach the photos to a message and send them to the number he put into my phone, with the text:

> Guess where I am right now?

Then I slide my phone into my pocket, sit back on the bench and admire the view for a while, trying not to constantly check for a response.

* * *

Kit

I've been coming to Kyoto Garden in London's Holland Park every day for the last week. Drawn here for some reason. I guess it's probably pretty obvious what that reason is.

And now I have the best reason of all – to see Chloe Dasher again. This time at her invitation.

I stroll through the grounds and make a beeline for the bench next to the koi pond that I'm pretty sure she must have been sitting on to take the pictures she sent me. I've spent a bit of time on that bench recently, thinking about the time we spent together in Japan and missing her.

I'd almost given up hope that she'd contact me, so the minute her message appeared on my phone I dropped everything I was doing and hared it over to the park in the hope she'd still be here.

I just had a *feeling* I'd be lucky.

And there she is, exactly where I imagined she'd be. Looking as serene and sexy as ever. She's staring into the depths of the pond as if her thoughts are a million miles away. Or maybe six thousand.

My heart is in my mouth as I walk quickly towards her, willing her to look up and see me.

'Hello, stranger,' I say, as she seems to sense me approaching and raises her head, her gaze meeting mine.

The look of delighted surprise on her beautiful face takes my breath away.

'I thought I was hallucinating there for a second,' she says, by way of reply.

I grin. 'Nope. It's really me. In the flesh. Bumping into you, on the other side of the world, after not seeing you for, what? A month?'

'Six weeks, three days, actually,' she says with a sheepish sort of smile.

'You've been counting?' I'm surprised, though delighted by this. It suggests she's been thinking about me as much as I've been thinking about her.

She shrugs. 'I just have a good memory for dates,' she says, but I see a tell-tale colour rise to her cheeks.

'So how have you been?' I ask.

'Oh, you know, surviving.'

We smile at each other awkwardly.

But I'm not going to let a bit of weirdness get in the way. I want this to work out too much. So I'm just going to launch straight in.

'Actually, I'm glad you got in contact,' I say, sitting down on the bench next to her. 'I'm setting up a charitable foundation to disseminate my wealth.' I quirk an eyebrow. 'How much money does one person need, right? And I was hoping I might be able to persuade you to consult for me. It'd be a fully paid gig, of course.'

'A foundation?' she says, looking stunned.

'Yeah. I want it to invest in protecting and re-establishing woodland in this country. I hear it needs a huge injection of cash and a concerted effort to reach the goals that have been set by 2030,' I say. 'As luck would have it, I currently have the means to do that. So I'm setting up a foundation to do it through.'

'Wow. I'm... lost for words. You really listened to what I said.'

'Yeah, I did. I listened, thought about it a lot after you'd gone and decided you were right. I need to use this obscene wealth I have for good. And you're right about something else too. I'm not built to be a billionaire. It's going to destroy me if I'm not careful.'

'Huh. Okay, well, good. The last thing I want is for you to be destroyed.'

'Thanks. That's good to hear,' I say with a smile.

'You're really going to give it all away?' she asks, as though she can't quite believe it.

'Well, most of it. I'll keep some back to help run my new start-up business venture and invest some for my future.'

'Right. Okay. Well, that's obviously amazing. I'm blown away to hear it. Good for you, Kit.'

'Thanks. You know, while I was travelling round Japan, once you'd left, it hit me that the things that have made me the happiest recently are things I've not paid for. They've been the spontaneous stuff. Things I'd not even imagined being on the cards. Like hanging out with you.'

Her eyes seem to spark at that, but there's wariness in her expression too.

'What does Katya think about the foundation?' she asks.

I shrug. 'No idea. I haven't spoken to her since she turned up at the hotel in Japan and I sent her packing.'

She sits up straighter. 'Oh! I just kind of assumed the two of you would get back together when she'd made the effort to travel all the way to the other side of the world to patch things up with you.'

I press my mouth into a line. 'Well, we didn't. I wasn't interested in working things out with her. There wasn't anything to work out, to be honest.'

'Oh.' She stares down at the ground. 'When you got that message from her it looked like you were really pleased to hear from her.'

I frown, remembering the fear that had rushed through me when I'd only read part of the messages, then the relief when they were just about her trying to reconciliate.

'I thought the message she sent was going to tell me she was pregnant, so I was smiling because I was so relieved she wasn't contacting me to say that. Just that she wanted to talk to me about getting back together.'

'Ohhhh,' she says on a long breath, then turns to flash me a look of embarrassment. 'I guess my head was so messed up after the wedding fiasco it triggered my fear of being out of the loop and rejected again. Sorry.'

'Understandable.' I'm actually relieved to hear this. It makes sense of why she left so abruptly.

'So it's completely over between you?' she asks.

'Yes,' I say with absolute confidence. 'I don't love her any more and I definitely don't want to get back together with her.'

She blinks rapidly at me. 'Oh. Right.' There are tears forming in her eyes and she turns away from me as if she's trying to get her emotions under control.

I turn away too, to give her a moment, and we both stare

ahead of us, towards the russet-coloured maple trees in the distance.

'How are you feeling about splitting with Adrian now?' I ask tentatively, after a tense moment of silence.

'Much better,' she says, shooting me a smile. 'I've come to realise that we weren't really that well suited. Not in the way I thought we were. Looking back, after having some space from it, I think we'd just got too *comfortable* with each other. I've always thought it would be great to marry your best friend because you'd never argue, never have those roller-coaster of emotions that can be so draining. Life would be peaceful and calm. But the truth is, there wasn't enough spark in our relationship to keep it alive. It was fizzling. Had been for a while. We didn't surprise or inspire each other and maybe you actually need that in a long-term relationship. To always be growing and evolving – alongside each other. And maybe arguments are good because they shake up the status quo and make you reassess how you feel about the other person and the direction you're both heading in.'

'And they can be hot,' I joke, flashing her a grin.

I can tell she's trying not to smile at that, but loses her fight. 'Trust you to say that,' she murmurs, rolling her eyes at me in mock antipathy.

I wave my hand at her in apology. 'Sorry, I interrupted.'

She lets out a breath. 'Anyway, in conclusion, I think we'd been set on a course neither of us wanted to change because of the emotional work it would have taken. It was just easier to stay together at the time.' She screws up her nose.

'But, when it came down to it, he was more willing to face the fact we weren't really that good together after all,' she adds. 'And then do something about it. I should probably be grateful to him for that. He's saved us both a lot of angst and a potentially stressful and expensive divorce.'

'Good of him,' I joke, though I actually mean that. Now he's out of the way I've got a fighting chance of getting her back.

She links her fingers together in her lap. 'The time I spent with you was great for forcing me to take stock and really think about what it is I want from life. You've always challenged me like that. Pushed my buttons and knocked me off course.'

'Well, like I say, if you fancy a new challenge, I'd love it if you'd consider helping me run my foundation. It could be alongside your current job if you decided you wanted to stay there.'

'Seriously?'

'Yep.'

'Wow, I don't know what to say.'

'Say yes.'

Turning away again, she stares out at the pond. 'Look, I really appreciate the offer. It's an amazing opportunity, seriously. But I have to be honest. I'm not sure I could work with you every day as a colleague and a friend because—' She swallows, then forces herself to finish the sentence. 'Because I've realised that I'm in love with you and it would be too hard to see you all the time and not be able to show you that.'

I let out a laugh of relief, and she turns to face me with confusion in her eyes.

'Jesus, Dasher. For fuck's sake, of course we'll be together as a couple,' I say, taking her trembling hands and gripping them hard. 'I love you too. Isn't that obvious? I thought it was obvious. What do you want me to do? Get down on one knee? Because I will if that's what you want. But if you'd rather partner up and see how it goes first, that's good for me too. As long as I get to be with you. That's all I care about.'

Her expression is one of relief now and, I'm relieved to see, happiness. 'You love me?'

'Of course I do. The feelings I had for you while we were together at uni never went away and they've only developed and intensified since we bumped into each other again. I think it was destiny that we both ended up in Kyoto together when we did. When we needed each other most. And we'd be crazy not to make the most of that luck. We'll just be picking up from where we left off five years ago. Adrian and Katya were just short diversions for a while.'

She raises one eyebrow at me. 'Not exactly short in my case.'

'Okay, fine. But you're missing my point.'

'I'm not. I'm just being argumentative, because it's hot,' she says, and gives me a slow wink.

Releasing her hands, I move them to cup her face instead and pull her towards me, kissing her firmly on the mouth.

She kisses me back and I bask in the familiar taste, scent, feel of her. This is exactly what I want. I'm absolutely certain about that.

'I'm not letting you go again. I'm *not* making that mistake a second time. We're clearly meant to be together,' I murmur against her lips.

Pulling back, I look her in the eyes. 'Fate threw us back together for a reason. Even if you think that's all bullshit, it doesn't matter. We're back in each other's lives now and I want it to stay that way. I love you. It feels *right* when I'm with you. It always did. I was just too young and green to trust that feeling before.'

'Like a baby lime,' she says with a grin.

Then *she* leans forward this time and presses her mouth to mine, sending a shiver of pleasure straight up my spine.

'Look, I understand why you freaked out and decided you

couldn't trust me,' I say when we break apart again, 'because of what happened with Adrian, but know this. I won't be looking for someone better because there *is* no-one better than you. Believe me, I've been looking for five years and was about to settle for someone less, but I'm so fucking glad that didn't work out. You're the only person I want to spend the rest of my life with. And I'd love it if you gave me the chance to prove it to you.'

'It might go wrong again,' she says in a gentle warning tone.

I shrug. 'Yeah. It might. No crystal balls, right? It'll be a work in progress.' I sit back, then reach over and take her hand in mine, linking our fingers together. 'I'm willing to put the work in. How about you?'

Nodding, she squeezes my hand.

'Yep. Ready and willing.'

My whole body floods with happiness at the lit-up expression on her face. 'Okay then. How about I ask you out on a proper date. We can start again from scratch.'

'I'd love to go on a date with you,' she says with a smile. 'I've got a feeling we're going to get on very well.'

'Great. Fancy going out for sashimi and adventures? I've been craving both since I last saw you in Kyoto.'

Her eyes light up. 'That sounds perfect.'

* * *

MORE FROM CHRISTY McKELLEN

Another spicy, sparkling, romantic read from Christy McKellen is available to order now here:

https://mybook.to/ChristyMcKellen11